THREE ME ꓓOR

D.E. HARKER

THREE MEN IN A MINOR

To Ruth and John.
(Bringing back memories
of Morris Minor motoring?)
Diana.

Matador
9 De Montfort Mews
Leicester LE1 7FW, UK
Tel: (+44) 116 255 9311 / 9312
Email: books@troubador.co.uk
Web: www.troubador.co.uk/matador

ISBN 978 1848760 554

British Library Cataloguing in Publication Data.
A catalogue record for this book is available from the British Library.

Typeset in 11pt Stempel Garamond by Troubador Publishing Ltd, Leicester, UK
Printed by the MPG Books Group in the UK

Matador is an imprint of Troubador Publishing Ltd

For my family

– and other Morris Minor enthusiasts to
celebrate the 60th anniversary of the iconic motor

Tribute is also paid to the inspiration of Jerome K. Jerome's
'Three Men in a Boat' (120 years young)
and John Buchan's 'The 39 Steps'.

ONE

'Bar None' was crowded as usual at this time of day and as usual, Rex, who worked only a stone's throw away in Lombard St., was late. By jutting out my elbows and standing astride, I managed to secure him a slender space but Fat Frank would have to take his chance.

'Hi!'

Frank's monstrously loud voice, perfected on the rugger pitch, cut across the din of animated crows (why does everyone wear black nowadays?) and optimistically I beckoned him over. The power of his voice had made him a natural for Falstaff in a school production and no doubt it now stood him in good stead teaching English at an Inner City Comprehensive, 'though it might more appropriately be called teaching English as a foreign language,' he always said.

At that moment, a group seated at a table by the door got up to leave and Frank was in there like a shot.

'God you look dreadful!' I said 'What's up?' The

three of us usually met once a month here – just a pie and pint – to air our grievances: 'the Unholy Trinity' we'd been called at school, but Frank hadn't turned up the first Tuesday in May and I'd been too busy to find out why.

We ordered some drinks and roast beef sandwiches and he explained. 'OFSTED' – Inspectors all over the bloody place I tell you. I'm thinking of packing it all in. Look at this' – he tugged at his shirt collar, which unusually seemed two sizes too large – and showed me three boils on his neck coming to a head. 'Stress.'

'You've lost some weight too. How's Victoria?' I asked, trying to cheer him up but it didn't.

'And that's another thing …'

I knew Frank ran a complicated love life – Victoria being a married colleague, whose husband also worked at the same school. Before he could tell all, Rex slipped into the spare seat with a groan 'What a morning – real crisis – you're lucky I could make it.' He took one of my sandwiches. 'Take over at Mid Yorks Water and I've landed myself in the middle of it.' He took a gulp of my beer. His mobile rang. He dealt with the caller, mentioning astronomical figures and obscure names, then turned to face us looking white and drained. He tried a smile 'How're things?' but he wasn't really interested.

'D'you know what I'd like? I'd like to be on a remote island … no cars … sun … no phones … no women … definitely no women …'

Rex was going through a nasty divorce from Kate, a volatile redhead with a fine line in revenge. She had an excellent job with Wigram Witherslade but was intent on taking Rex to the cleaners.

'Desolation Island?' I suggested trying to lighten the atmosphere and I told one or two stories about some of the odd clients we had currently at the architectural practice where I worked in Wigmore St, among them a scandalous one about Count Humberto, who claimed to be of Royal blood and who I'd hoped would want us to design a palace instead of a loft conversion, but they still looked preoccupied although Frank managed a short, barking sort of laugh.

Well, I had my worries too,– mainly concerned with Olivia's schooling. Jane and I had had quite a few arguments on this subject lately, Jane stressing that although Livvie was only 18 months, we'd probably left it too late to get her into Sandlings, which would be the gateway to the pre-prep Abbeyford and thence via interviews and tests to St Jane's junior and, exams being passed, to St Jane's. This sounded like too much pressure to me. I broached the subject to Frank and Rex but they gave blank, uncomprehending stares.

'Remember those holidays we used to go on – my God it must be nearly 20 years ago now – The Inter-rails, the Norfolk Broads. The time I took my mother's old Morris Minor to Cornwall and it kept breaking down – happy days.' I'd ordered another drink and we all raised our glasses – 'Happy days' but we sounded melancholy.

'Don't look now, but guess who's just walked in,' Rex said. We didn't have to look – and kept our heads down. Ben Price-Kettle had dogged our footsteps since school days, never believing that he wasn't one of our best friends, never realising how much we disliked him. He was the original freeloader – attaching himself to people, using them, dropping them. This way, he had insinuated himself into a media job through a girl-friend who he'd then discarded, shared an expensive spread in Docklands with someone who was abroad most of the time, and holidayed and partied wherever he could insinuate himself with his dubious charm. He was good looking in a weak sort of way. With a bit of luck, he'd be rumbled one day.

Half turning my head, I saw him weave his way to the far end of the bar and greet an expensively dressed woman with freakishly cut black hair who looked vaguely familiar.

'It's all right – he didn't see us.' I said.

'Must be off – shouldn't be here at all, really.' Frank heaved himself out of his chair.

'Neither should I,' Rex said with a grim smile. His mobile rang again.

'Why don't you turn it off?'

He gave me a pitying look.

'Why don't we, the three of us, go off together somewhere – just for 2 or 3 days, like we used to?' I knew I was crazy saying such a thing but just for a moment a desperate gleam of hope came into their eyes.

'Why don't we?' I persisted.

'Impossible,' Frank said. Rex answered his phone.

'No, it's not, mid July – you'll be on holiday then.'

'I usually go up to Shropshire to see my parents then. I half planned to take Victoria…..'

'Come on – none of that's set in stone. Jane wants

to visit her sister in Canada sometime with Livvie.' We both looked at Rex. He was cursing under his breath. 'Must dash – cheers.'

'How about mid July – a few days – away from it all...'

'You must be joking. With the load I've got on at the moment?'

'Fix it,' I said 'You need it. Believe me. We needn't go far. Any suggestions?' I was thinking of Herefordshire and a nice little riverside pub where Jane and I had spent a weekend before Livvie was born.

Rex stood up.

'D'you know....' Frank's voice had become unusually mellow. 'We once had a holiday in Galloway when I was about 10. Never forgotten it.... Fishing, walking, golf, castles.... peace, quiet.... we walked up a hill on a Bank Holiday and there was no one else.... *No one else –*'

'Well yes. That sounds *just* the sort of place – the simple life.' This was encouraging.

'*What* sort of place?' I felt an arm round my shoulder. 'Sorry I didn't come over right away, 'Ben Price-Kettle apologised, 'I had to congratulate Laurel Rhodes on that piece about her in "Hello!".'

The vaguely familiar face had been that of a holiday programme presenter on Olympia television.

'*What* sort of place?' he repeated.

'Galloway,' Rex replied without thinking.

'Great, when are we off?' Ireland, isn't it?'

'Scotland. I've always loved that book by John Buchan, "The 39 Steps", but they never get the story right when they film it. Did you know that?' Frank was well away now and had a far away look in his eye.

'Right, so Scotland it is. Did you know my middle name's Chatten?' We didn't. 'Just e-mail me all the details,' and Ben took leave of us.

We broke up after that.

'I'll phone you at home,' I said to Frank. Home for Frank was a cupboard in Kensington.

'Mid July,' I reminded Rex.

'No way.' Home for Rex was a one-room studio flat in North London.

Home for me, Jane and Livvie was a converted garage in Richmond and as I travelled home that night, Hammersmith and the crowded tube vanished in a Highland mist and in its place was somewhere I'd never been – a glen with shining river, moorland, bracken, peat – oh those whisky ads. There was a rush of air as the doors opened. Someone nearby was eating a highly spiced take-away but the smell evaporated to be replaced by wafts of heather blowing on a warm breeze. Does heather smell? I'm sure it does.

TWO

We had grilled Scottish salmon for supper that night and although it was masked by pesto sauce, it seemed to be some sort of sign.

'You know, I'm sure Livvie could try for a scholarship at some stage – she's very bright.' Jane kicked off.

I said you couldn't really assess a child's academic ability at 18 months and besides, I was totally against all kind of pressure and so the usual heated discussion / row started up but catching a genuine taste of salmon for a second, I became calm, reasonable 'maybe you have something.' Jane gave me a hard stare.

'You know that trip you were thinking of taking to see Anna – I saw a cheap flight offered, month of July. We could scrape enough for you and Livvie to go, couldn't we?'

Her right eyebrow went up. 'What about you?'

'Might spend a quiet weekend with Frank and Rex –

They're both stressed out – it would do them good – a bit of hill walking…..'

….'A bit of drinking…. I can imagine – Francis Hummell and Rex King can booze for Britain.'

'We're sober citizens now.' But she didn't seem too concerned.

'Would you really be alright? It would be wonderful. Anna's longing to see Livvie!'

I was feeling magnanimous 'Go for 3 weeks – it's not worth going all that way for less.'

'That would be brilliant' She leant over and gave me a kiss.

The evening turned out to be very pleasant.

***

I found a moment at the office the next day to send an e-mail to Rex and left a message on Frank's answer phone suggesting they come to my place for a pizza a week on Friday, 9 p.m. to discuss further plans. I was sure Frank was three-quarters convinced but Rex would be an uphill job. He e-mailed back 'what plans? Anyway will be in Hong Kong. Byeee.' I persevered and eventually hit on a date and time, limited in Rex's case, to suit.

Jane was out discussing compression socks and DVT preventative exercises with her friend, the much travelled Clemmie, and Livvie was tucked up and asleep when they arrived.

'You've got such a lot of space here' Frank stretched his large frame, his arms touching both sides of the kitchen at the same time. I thought he was being sarcastic until I remembered his own pad.

I opened a bottle of Chianti Classico and Frank spread out an elderly Ordnance Survey map of Galloway he'd found somewhere. We pored over it and discovered some interesting names in the area – Murder Hole, Hogs of Borgan, Loch Dungeon, Bloody Mires – places that might bear further inspection. Dalmellington – there was poetry in that name. Then we sat back on our heels.

'Look, I may as well tell you,' Frank said looking miserable. 'Victoria and I have had a hell of a row. She and Hugh are thinking of applying for jobs in Birmingham – she said it could be a new start for their relationship – they'd been through a bad patch but a move to Birmingham could make all the difference........ And there was I thinking...'

I refilled his glass.

The pizzas arrived and half an hour after that, Rex arrived. He'd had a lift with someone called Sonia and there'd been a serious hold up at Kew'

'Queue at Kew in fact' he didn't bother to laugh but lit a cigarette. He was wound up tight as an alarm clock. Frank seemed to have cheered up a bit and laughed more than my little joke had merited. I'd found a bottle of wine Jane had won in a raffle and it wasn't bad. We ate our pizzas and Frank showed us how the boil population on his neck had increased. 'Stress. I'm burnt out!'

We compared notes and discovered we were all suffering from severe lack of sleep, tension in the neck muscles, migraines and intermittent impotency. Rex said he'd tried yoga but when the instructor had asked him to imagine floating to the top of a very high tree, as a sufferer from vertigo, he'd become dizzy and anxious; I'd tried jogging and occasional games of squash and Frank ate.

'I had 31 e-mails to answer the other morning and the 32nd was from that scumbag Ben Price-Kettle saying 'so when are we off to Scotland? I binned it' Rex said.

I'd had just the same message and so had Frank on his answer phone.

There was definitely something seductive about the 'off to Scotland' bit and after topping up our glasses– Rex had produced a decent Sancerre – I came straight to the point.

'Off to Scotland – that's where we're thinking of going – *all* of us – minus Ben P-K of course' Rex with a nervous spasm, flicked his ash over Jane's pile of school prospectii but they didn't catch fire. 'Look – we're all in desperate need of a break. Jane's going to visit her sister, Frank's off for six weeks and you must have a back log of holidays due – when did you last take one. I'm being serious.'

'It's not easy – presentations to make… A huge corporate bonding do coming up' Rex was hedging but I stood firm. 'Mid July. The 3 of us – the simple outdoor life – plain good food … fresh air'

'I'm a country person at heart' Frank chipped in, sounding soulful 'Always have been'…

'It'll be just like old times' I went on and to ram the point home to Rex 'you can switch off your mobile and forget about that bitch, Kate.'

'I don't know.' Rex was weakening – he made a last

stand 'I've some serious dental work pending too' but this was pathetic.

Frank straightened out the old map again… 'We've got to Gatehouse of Fleet via Castle Douglas. Ah, I remember having a picnic near Archibald the Grim's Castle – delicious – we had…'

'Iced buns and lashings of ginger beer' Rex – sotto voce.

…'And we found'…

'Hidden treasure, I know'

'Shut up and stop being so negative' I was getting tired of Rex's attitude. 'It may not be as far flung as Hong Kong or as exotic as Mauritius (this last was meant to sting as it was where Rex and Kate had honeymooned) but it's peaceful, accessible and looks ideal for what we need. I'm going to do some sketching – for pleasure – away from the drawing board.'

'I shall follow in the footsteps of Richard Hannay' Frank announced grandly 'and a bit of fishing and golf – rough shooting.'

We looked at Rex.

'What would you do, with all the time in the world?' I asked him and was taken aback when he told us that he intended to write an opera.

'Not the music, you understand – the libretto. Something on the lines of Wagner's Ring Cycle.'

This was admirable: no point in starting in a small way.

'All those Germanic myths and legends woven into a political polemic issue. Well, why not an English version…. The Simple Sword of Truth and the Trusty

Shield…. (was he getting mixed up with something else?) Arthurian tales, 'the Faerie Queen,' Robin Hood for God's sake!' He was getting quite worked up. We were impressed.

'You should go for it' Frank said.

'Definitely… it's your duty really – you owe it to yourself.'

'I know' his eyes were moist.

'You just need time to yourself' – he was nearly there.

We went on to discuss transport – Frank offered up his mother's Morris Minor – still taxed and licensed after all these years – but this would need some consideration – the route, where to stay – pubs, do bed and breakfast or camp (camp?)… we decided a mix of all three. We even discussed clothes – those hunky shirts and trousers seen in catalogues… and boots.

'Could be cold in Scotland.'

'And wet.'

There was nearly a row when I said 'No television, no newspapers, no women.'

We remembered the job of planning our trips of long ago – the gadgets taken and never used – and the old enthusiasm returned. We even drank a toast with the remains of some Scotch I found.

'Scots wha hae!'

We didn't know what it meant but it sounded totally appropriate. 'Scots wha hae!' we shouted.

Rex put his hand to his ear. 'What was that?'

'What?' I asked.

'That noise.'

'It's Livvie.'

'Livvie?' They'd forgotten.

'Christ, is that the time?' Rex consulted his watch and asked if I'd phone for a taxi for the two of them – he was staying the night with someone called Simon 'helluva decent guy' who lived in Gloucester Road.

THREE

I was half afraid that Rex might have forgotten he'd virtually agreed to join us on our break but he hadn't. In fact he said it might suit him very well to 'disappear' for a few days in July – whether this was something to do with Kate, Corporate bonding or some deal which had gone wrong and for which he might be blamed, was not at the time clear.

We'd managed to stretch the 'few days' into 10. Frank, without consulting us, said his mother would be pleased to let us use her ancient Morris Minor 'it would do it good to have a long run'.….. hmmmm. His parents would be away on a safari holiday in Africa but would send the key and fill it up with petrol and we'd drive up to Shrewsbury in Rex's Saab convertible – soon to be sold.

Excited messages passed between us concerning kit, itinerary, reading matter – Frank was taking Buchan, of course; I favoured one of Ian Rankin's pacey novels dealing with the seedy under belly of Edinburgh (a million miles from the Scottish scenario *we* were hoping for). Rex had no time for such trivia – booking one or two nights at B & Bs – tricky one this due to widespread lack of fax, e-mail facilities and answer phones in the area.

I managed to borrow a camping stove from my godson, Paris, who was off to Sardinia. 'I've never used it, actually' he said. I didn't tell him it had been a present from me.

'We can pick up an old tent I have from my parents' said Frank. Hmmm… I was beginning to wonder how simple this simple life was going to be.

***

I was very busy before we left, working overtime to satisfy clients that they weren't about to be neglected and didn't return home until late in the evenings. Just as well as the house felt empty without Jane and Livvie. I missed them. I was ready to be on my way and so was Frank who was feeling depressed. He and Victoria had split up. I don't believe Rex seriously believed he was going anywhere – surely it would be impossible for him to take time off for *leisure* of all things, wouldn't it? But on the appointed day, and only an hour late, he picked us up with all our belongings including Frank's gun, golf clubs, an inflatable rubber dinghy, my easel, wet weather gear, cold weather gear, the camping stove and a fold-away picnic table for 4 also never before used – a present to Rex from Kate in happier days.

We sped out of Richmond, up the M1 and headed North to the accompaniment of an old 'Stones' number very loud. Rex's mobile beeped twice. I was planning to do something about this later on but didn't want to upset him while he was driving.

'Did either of you hear any more from Ben?' he shouted. We both shouted 'Yes.'

'He definitely got wind of something. Remember when he tagged along with us on that cycling tour of the War graves? He didn't even bring his bike!'

'*Or* many francs and fools that we were, we stumped up for him to hire one.' I yelled. 'And he'd managed to break one of the pedals.'

Frank was a large brooding presence, hunched miserably in the front passenger seat but managed to rouse himself once in Shropshire, to give Rex some directions.

'There's a decent pub about a couple of miles away – how about an early lunch.'

'Good idea.' I had cramp in my left leg and didn't like the way the barrel of Frank's gun was jammed, pointing at the back of my head.

Rex made 3 phone calls at 'The Grapes.'

We emerged feeling refreshed. Already London was an alien planet, to me at any rate.

Opposite, people were pushing their way out of the Village Hall, staggering under the weight of bundles. A large poster, in crude letters read 'ANYTHING GOES' – sale in aid of church roof restoration fund.' It looked an historic old church – 17th century – so when Frank suggested putting his nose round the door of the Hall, I didn't object to donating 50p entrance fee. I came out pretty quickly and went to have a closer look at the church.

Ten minutes later Rex was revving up the engine impatiently.

Frank came out of that Hall beaming. He held up an enormous pair of tweed plus fours.

'You can't be serious' Rex said 'those are gross. What the hell d'you think you're going to do with them?'

'They're just the job. Look!' They had braces.

'I'm not going to be seen anywhere near you. Plus there's no room for another thing.'

But I could see that the tweed plus fours had made Frank happy at some level and that had to be a good thing. We folded them up as best we could and I sat on them until we got to 'Applegarth.'

***

'There she is' Frank opened the garage door. Rex and I caught each other's eye. 'Grand old girl. Showing … 8,400.' Then he explained quickly, 'Three times around the clock of course! Ageless in her way.'

The old girl was dark green, had a divided front windscreen and the familiar, hopeful number plate TRY. 'Age shall not wither her – nor custom stale her infinite variety' he quoted and that was the worry. She had an infinite variety of naughty tricks. She was a wicked old girl with dodgy brakes, draughts, serious lack of acceleration when most needed…. I could go on. Luckily she had a roof rack. Frank produced the key, reversed her with a roar of the engine and Rex reluctantly drove his Saab into the garage.

It took an hour to re-pack. Frank had discovered a note from his mother on the back seat, with kindly warnings about damp and shell fish – together with a large tin containing a fruit cake – great but where to put it – and a hairy tweed jacket, which Frank greeted like a dear old friend.

'You'll have to wear it' we told him. It was a warm day but he had to, he was already sitting on a pile of sweaters and some waterproof gear.

We juddered off with much revving and full choke.

'Just smell the leather. This is real driving.' Well he was getting into the right spirit.

To deaden the sound of his barbecue flavour crisps and crunchie bar munching, Rex suggested a tape. He'd forgotten. No tape deck but Radio 4 was finally found and until we reached the M6, we listened to an account of a woman's hysterectomy. Frank was proud of the reception and had it on full volume.

It was quite a comfort to recognise one of Frank's old foibles – the constant snacking. I'd just begun to wonder if this 'away from it all' thing was going to work. I mean – who were these guys? What did I really know of them now? I might have been sitting with a couple of complete strangers. This was the longest I'd been with either of them for years. Twenty years ago as spotty adolescents, a bond of mild anarchy at school had held us together; we'd shared a few miseries and even less triumphs, but now? Meeting for the odd drink from time to time we spent the 30 minutes simultaneously grumbling and not really listening to each other. What did they know of some of my weird clients, the frustrations and hell of planning committees, my longing to grow vegetables? Why was Rex finding it handy to 'disappear' for a few days? Was he seeing anyone? Why the hell did Frank keep a shotgun in London? What were their views on religion, politics, drugs, birth control? This whole thing could be a horrible mistake.

Perhaps we were all having doubts. The weather had clouded over. Frank snapped off a talk on primary education, which I might have found interesting and we fell into a silence. I think we'd have even been grateful for the ring of Rex's mobile. There didn't seem to be anything to talk about until Frank said.

'Think of all those poor sods trying to get home from work now' and that cheered us up.

***

FOUR

I nodded off from time to time but in the end, prickly heat from the plus fours underneath got to me. We'd been travelling up the motorway for about 3½ hours and had turned off on to an A road towards Dumfries. It was not a comfortable ride and the slower pace, instead of giving us a sense of unwinding only gave us time to brood. I was feeling guilty about jobs left undone, especially seeing to the strengthening of the Count's new roof garden. He'd asked me to call him Jim recently but I feared we might soon revert to more formal terms.

Frank was on to Munchy Wotsits now and Rex, between cigarettes, had developed a twitch – a sharp jerk upwards of his right hand to ear – mobile deprivation.

The itching intensified. Were there fleas in those old plus fours? I suddenly had a craving for a piece of that fruitcake. Could the tin be located?

We had to slow down for some road works and I

noticed a brown sign pointing to the left 'Caerlaverock Castle.' We were speeding up again.

'Turn left!' I shouted 'Look– it's Ca – Caer – that Castle. I've always wanted to see it.' This was a lie, I'd never heard of it.

Frank swerved just in time and swore as we heard something shifting on the roof.

'What is all this? It'll take us miles out of our way.'

'Not necessarily' I replied smoothly. 'We really shouldn't miss it.' I hoped it wouldn't be just a pile of stones. 'Anyway, we need a break.'

It wasn't too far. We came over the bank with the Solway estuary beyond and there it was.

'Yes!' I punched the air. (Well the 2 inches of space I had above my head.)

'I see what you mean' said Frank.

The twin-towered gatehouse of the Castle stood proud and magnificent surrounded by a moat. There were seductive glimpses of a ruined 17th Century building in Renaissance style of the same soft pink sandstone grafted on to the walls. It was a gem. I could have spent a day there but it was nearly 6 p.m. and a sign said it closed at 6.30.

We parked, had a quick and hungry attack on the fruitcake, which we hacked at with my old Swiss army knife….. cracks were already appearing in the thin veneer of our suave urban façade.

Then I whipped out a sketchpad and pencil from my pocket. Frank went to find the Gents and Rex said he'd buy a brochure or was he going off to send a text message?

I was working against time but lost in the novelty of

doing something for my own pleasure when I happened to glance at the bridge. There was Frank staring moodily into the moat – that was o.k. but nearby, Rex was chatting up a girl, blonde and beautiful, heads together. What was this? Our first stop North of the border and he was already breaking rule number one. Next thing, they'd be swapping 'phone numbers.

I leapt out of the car and shouted to Frank. 'We'd better be on our way' pointing at my watch. Rex didn't hear. I ran over to where he and the girl were now lounging back against the masonry, laughing together.

'Time to go.'

He looked surprised to see me. 'Alice works with N.Y. Carrington Marvel. She's staying at a big house not a million miles from here.' I gave a curt nod.

'Must be off' pointed again at my watch.

'What's the rush?'

'You know Mrs Douglas wants us to clock in before 7. We're not going to make it as it is.'

As if to reinforce my rather weak excuse, a bell rang.

'I guess I must be going too' she said. She was with a small party and they were beckoning.

She and Rex gave each other wistful looks and she gave a little shrug of her shoulders, a smile that said 'what a pity' and went to join her friends.

'So, what's this all about then?' Rex said furiously as we went back to the car. 'Correct me if I'm wrong but isn't this meant to be a carefree, stress busting, leave our watches behind sort of trip? What the hell d'you mean by busting in like that?' He looked mean and angry. I wasn't sure I even liked him – had ever liked him.

'Right' I said and explained again in simple language, the inflexible charter we'd drawn up for our break.

'Do you know, I was humming a snatch of Prokofiev and she recognised it and joined in.'

'That doesn't make you soul mates' I said.

We glared at each other.

As we drove off, Rex was muttering 'Alice Van Heck' and pressing his mobile. 'Alice Van Heck.' He was doing this to annoy me.

Luckily, Frank had found a minute or two to talk to a guide at the Castle who'd given him a brief outline of its history which he now passed on to us and this broke the brooding silence.

Apparently, with its situation, close to the shore of the Solway in Border country, Caerlaverock Castle had been constructed as an English bridgehead for possible invasion of Scotland in the 13th century. There were sieges and strife between the two countries and then it had come into the ownership of the Maxwell family. A period of tranquillity when James VI of Scotland became also James 1st of England encouraged Robert Maxwell, in bullish mood to incorporate into the buildings, a rather grand new house – a glaringly different structure from the defensive ones. A 17th century fashion statement – a house built for show.

Then it was the old, old story – problems with that highhanded monarch, Charles I. Not with Cromwell this time but the covenanters. Another siege and another Robert Maxwell dream gone up in a puff of smoke. Thereafter, the Castle remained a ruin. I promised myself to go back one day.

We drove into the centre of Dumfries, passing solid sandstone villas and stopped at the Station Hotel for a quick pint and bacon sandwich in the bar noting the local accent going on all around. Rex was still a wee bit sulky but I didn't care. Right was on my side. He wasn't going to ruin our holiday with his selfish habits. A television was playing somewhere and he wandered off.

'You from London then?' An elderly couple out partying with another elderly couple had obviously taken pity on two Sassenachs placing our order in an alien tongue, friendless in a foreign land.

'Yes, we are'

'Going on a wee tour?'

'Yes, we are.'

'Whereabouts would ye be staying?'

'Gatehouse of Fleet'

'Och. I ken it weel. Ma grandmother minded the time when the old queen came visiting. She said the coastal road from Cardoness to Creetown was the most beautiful in the whole of the British Isles.'

'Aye, she did.'

'Old Queen Mary?' I asked, thinking I should contribute something.

'No, no, Queen Victoria.'

Frank who'd been sunk in gloom, started at this name. I quickly changed the subject.

'Great hotel you've got here.'

'Aye, thanks to the age of steam. Railways, you see and all these grand hotels sprung up. They were great builders, the Victorians – aye, great builders.'

Frank couldn't stand any more: he vanished behind a copy of 'The Catering Times' he'd found in a corner.

***

I seriously thought Rex might jump on the next train south, seeing we were at a station but although looking grim, he got into the car. As we drove out of town past a statue of Robert Burns, over and into the country, he started to tell us what he'd seen on the television news. I didn't want to know. Then Frank's mobile began to ring.

'Switch the bloody thing off!' I shouted.

We passed a small loch on the right.

'Stop the car! Switch it off!'

'But it might be...'

'Tough' I said. 'Listen – we agreed before we set off...' and I gave them a hard time, then softened them up using the old technique I employ to awkward clients who rubbish my ideas. 'Look, these are the facts and your infinite intelligence and good sense will be bound to make us agree, after all you have integrity, imagination, enlightenment'... and ...

The loch had given me an idea. We'd have a solemn ceremony. I explained it to them. After a minute, Frank agreed 'O.k., o.k. I suppose it makes sense.' We looked at Rex who, to my surprise, said 'Oh, what the hell. Come on then.'

Ceremoniously, we went to the edge of the loch, raised our mobiles above our heads and flung them in. Frank's was an old model – and as it flew through the air, it started to ring again: it entered the water with a splash and an eerie sound that was a cross between a shriek and a cry for help – not a sound you'd like to hear if you were alone in an old, dark house in the wee small hours – rang out, then silence.

Rex gave a nervous, high-pitched laugh. I started laughing and then Frank, who'd looked appalled at the death throes of his mobile started in with his loud bray. We fell about and it was as if the cork had been yanked out of a huge bottle of fizz. For the first time in years, I saw us as we'd been 20 years ago.

Everyone needs a good laugh from time to time.

FIVE

'We're running out of petrol' Frank sounded good-natured again.

'Mrs Douglas was expecting us at 7.' Rex was positively laid back.

It was now 9 o'clock.

I, however, felt tense and worried – I always prided myself on my promptness and now we'd flung our 'phones away, there was no way of contacting her. This was not strictly true as I'd deftly stuffed a few odds and ends I'd found in my pocket into my mobile case before chucking it into the loch and the mobile itself was safe in another pocket. Well I might want to contact Jane, mightn't I? I felt fully justified but I wasn't about to confess.

We found a petrol station eventually. It was open and I eased myself out, offering to pay. Frank asked me to throw in a cracknel bar for him and Rex came to top up his cigarette supply. I sorted out the money.

'Don't do that' Rex said jabbing me in the ribs. I knew what it was, I'd come out with an 'Och' quite involuntarily on finding I'd no small change.

'We could 'phone Mrs Douglas from here' Frank said.

Great idea but I, who'd organised the B & B, couldn't find either her number or her address. I must have had it in the pocket among the stuff I'd used for ballast..... it was now in the loch. Brilliant!

I managed to assume a vagueness and they weren't too bothered but as the road wound down the hill into Gatehouse of Fleet, they didn't seem too pleased either.

'Pull in here' I suggested. In the gathering dusk I could see the wide main street of an attractive small town and on the left, behind a clock tower, a whitewashed hotel. It looked inviting.

'We'll have a drink and ask. Everyone knows everyone in an area like this.'

I'd remembered a bit more.... 'Craig' something, or was it 'Crag?'

At the cosy bar, we ordered a wee dram or two of the wine of the country and asked the barman about a Mrs Douglas of Craig or Crag whatever. A couple of farmers, having a quiet grumble about the dry, sunny weather, which apparently was no good for something or other and some fishermen grumbling about the lack of river and loch water, stopped talking.

'Och, that'll be Mungo and Pat – Upper Craig Farm.'

What we hadn't realised was that we were in Douglas country and immediately, heated discussions, arguments even, broke out. Various permutations on Douglas,

Craig or Crag were proffered. Isobel and Jim Douglas of 'Craig Lockhart' seemed to be the favourite, followed by Mungo and Pat.

'Do they all do bed and breakfast?' I asked.

There was silence, then someone said to me accusingly 'You never mentioned anything about bed and breakfast.' They were quite hostile now.

'Well, thanks anyway, guys – I'm pretty sure it was the first ones you mentioned.' I just wanted to get out.

'Mungo and Pat' the barman said triumphantly.

'*I* didn't know they'd started doing B & B' one of the fishermen said bitterly. 'They didn't tell *me*.'

'Well, there you go…. That's Mungo and Pat for you' and I jostled Rex and Frank and nodded towards the door.

'Thank God you got that sorted out' Frank said but I had to explain that I hadn't.

Fortunately there was a telephone directory on the Reception desk and I spotted 'O Douglas, Higher Black Crag, Station Road' and it looked familiar.

It took rather a long time to find the house in the dark. Mrs O Douglas, when we eventually roused her, said she'd given us up but we'd better come in. She was dour and I didn't blame her.

Was it only this morning we left London? I was given a child's room with teddy bears on the windowsill. Frank was still fiddling about with his golf clubs, gun etc. thinking they'd be unsafe if left outside, forgetting this wasn't the wicked city and Rex had followed Mrs Douglas to some remote part of the house. I could hear their footsteps receding. I then heard Frank pounding up a further flight of stairs and going into a room directly above mine. There was a thundering crash as he plonked all his belongings on the floor.

One of the teddy bears had a worried expression. I picked him up and thought about Livvie.

Later, there was a knock at the door and Frank popped his head round. He gave a look of concern.

'You o.k.?'

I was still hugging the bear and no doubt looked melancholy.

'Breakfast at eight, I gather. Look, you know I promised to read a chapter of 'The 39 Steps' aloud each evening.' He became apologetic 'would you mind if I give it a miss tonight…. It's rather late, all that driving…. Sorry.'

'Don't worry, don't worry.'

'I'll do two chapters tomorrow'…….

'Good night, Frank.'

It was very late and by the time he'd stopped fighting with his golf clubs overhead, returned from the bathroom and tested the springs on his bed I was more than ready to drop off but Frank, as I remembered, does a particularly frightening line in snoring with savage crescendos followed by sad whimpers.

***

I opted for a simple breakfast of cereal, toast and tea and Rex, when he appeared, fancied an even simpler one of tomato juice and black coffee but he had to settle for orange juice. Frank came into the dining room about half an hour later and asked for 'the full Scottish breakfast' and 'I hope you've got some condensed milk' he said.

'Condensed milk?' Mrs Douglas asked faintly.

'For my porridge.'

She shuddered and shook her head sadly but we looked shocked when she said, as she put a huge plate of bacon, egg, sausage, fried bread and haggis in front of Frank 'Bye the way, someone rang up last night asking for you.'

We looked at each other stupefied.

'It was late when he rang – I said you weren't here, which was true. I wrote down his name somewhere.

'Och!' was all I could say. Rex gave me a hard stare.

'Here it is' she held up a scrap of paper and on it was written, 'Price-Kettle.' 'Said it was important you 'phone him. He sounded really nice, mind… really friendly.' We chalked up a black mark in our landlady's book as we simultaneously said 'Yeah!' sarcastically and I screwed up the piece of paper and threw it into the waste paper basket.

We argued among ourselves as to who had let slip the 'phone number of one of the two B & B's we'd booked into. The others said they hadn't mentioned it to anyone. Hadn't that been part of the scheme – so that no one could contact us? I had suggested it myself and had only told Jane's mother in case she needed to get in touch.

'Surely he couldn't have rung *her*' but I realised that was just the sort of thing Ben would do. Finding out the number of a Mrs B. Priestley, who lived in a village near Haywards Heath and spinning her some yarn, could be typical.

Accusing eyes were on me.

'He'll hound us down' Frank said.

'Sorry, really sorry. Who'd have thought he'd have sunk so low?

'I would' said Rex 'and he'll ruin everything.' This was true 'and anyway, how's he able to take off on holiday at a moment's notice. What's this marvellous job he's clawed his way up to in the media for God's sake?' Frank said he thought it was something to do with funding or placements or something but no one really knew.

We'd half wondered if we should stay on at Mrs Douglas's for an extra night but this settled it – we'd have to cover our tracks.

The 'phone started ringing in the hall, which caused Rex to jerk his arm violently – he was still suffering from withdrawal symptoms – and his cup of black coffee was liberally dispersed over table cloth, carpet and down a photo frame containing the likeness of, presumably, the late Mr Douglas giving him a sudden and unpleasant scar.

Mrs Douglas, coming back into the dining room after speaking – and we listened with bated breath to her chat with the local minister about some church matter, took in the new design on the table cloth and pre-empted any idea we might have had about staying on. 'I have some more guests arriving…' she looked at her watch 'in about half an hour, so if you'd….' and she was fully booked up for the next 2 weeks, she said 'Yes, really busy.'

Carrying his gun, golf clubs and overnight bag down the stairs, Frank managed to knock a small jug of flowers off a landing windowsill.

It was good to be out in the open air.

The white road snaked away up into the moorland and looked inviting. Already, at 10 o'clock it was hot and I was glad to be wearing old khaki shorts: I noticed Frank had decided against the tweed plus fours.

When we'd reassembled our luggage, we drove back into the town and bought some basic ingredients for a picnic. We then headed off up towards the moors and distant blue hills, past estates, fields with grazing belted Galloway cattle, a rushing river on the right and a sturdy tower house, which I'd liked to have sketched but Frank had his own agenda and our first stop had to be the old Gatehouse Station.

'Somewhere along this railway track, Richard Hannay got off the Dumfries train' he said, as if talking of a real person... 'and at one of the stations existing at the time. It could be Gatehouse – and I quite favour this as Cairnsmore of Fleet' (he waved his hand vaguely in the direction of an impressive range of high hills to the North) 'is mentioned later when he doubles back, or it could be the remote Loch Skerrow Halt or perhaps boggy Mossdale. I'm not going to be drawn into an argument on this one.'

This suited us perfectly well as it was obvious that we had not the slightest idea of what he was talking about.

'What really matters' he continued ' is that it was on this track somewhere, so we'll park just here and walk the length.'

He pulled up by what had once been the station and stationmaster's cottage. Over to the right, a huge viaduct with towering arches rose up over the shallow river. This classical, man-made structure was in sharp contrast to the natural scenery. It could have been Roman, a 'Pont du Fleet.' Very sketchable.

SIX

So anyway there we were, ready to start operation 'wind down.' We, most used to cement, concrete and tarmac were about to tread the springy turf, bracken and heather dodging snakes, in our various walking boots. Mine were new, Rex's borrowed and Frank's – his father's and a size too small.

There was a self-consciousness about us as we adjusted rucksacks, full of nothing very much and then we looked at each other critically but, feeling benevolent, I didn't tell Rex how weird he looked in his all black gear. Frank had gone to the other extreme.

I took a deep breath – the air was sweet and pure – the heather and bracken *did* smell – sweet and dry. No petrol or diesel fumes polluted it and I felt a great shaking off of worries and responsibilities and even caught some of Frank's enthusiasm for Hannay as he outlined our route on the map.

'That hat you're wearing' Rex said to me 'does nothing for you.'

I wanted to stop and make a sketch of the majestic viaduct but Frank was eager to get going and we joined the track and started off towards it into the hills and forestry plantations. I ignored Rex's rude remark about my hat.

As we stepped out, I thought how different this was to my only other experience of Scotland, which had been a brief and completely urban one.... A winter visit to Glasgow as a student with three others, to worship at the shrines of Charles Rennie Mackintosh – even taking Earl Grey and scones at Miss Cranston's Tea Rooms. Having been sadly unappreciated in his lifetime, his reputation nowadays has soared to the extent of ultimate celebrity status – by having a shopping centre named after him. Cities, traffic, noise, all so far removed from the wild, silent country surrounding us now.

Coming to the part of the old railway track which passed over the viaduct, Rex suddenly remembered he had no head for heights. By crawling along on his hands and knees and with ingenious use of Frank's belt as a dog lead, we managed to drag and coerce him across. I brought up the rear shouting cries of encouragement and 'Don't look down' and the occasional kick when he threatened to stop. Luckily there was no one to see this charade but it was another 'lost sketch' opportunity.

'For God's sake, give me a drink' Rex cried when we reached the other side. He took a swig of whisky from my silver flask and I hoped there was nothing more sinister than alcohol in it as it hadn't been used since I'd received it as a 21st birthday present. We all took two or three gulps as we pressed on into the hills. It grew very hot and I was glad of my hat. Rex had to improvise headgear with a dark purple handkerchief, which he knotted 'Blackpool dad' style and altogether he now resembled a dusty black widow spider with his long, thin limbs and unpleasant expression.

'How about an early lunch?' Frank suggested presently. This sounded like an excellent idea and we found a rocky outcrop on the moors.

Bread and cheese– Lockerbie Cheddar'…. *Lockerbie* Cheddar? How come?– had never tasted so good and we washed it down with cans of warm lager. Then there was the remains of the fruitcake. We felt drowsy after this

The cheerful sound of grasshoppers and the occasional moorland bird were soporific. I sank back into the bracken and watched the scudding clouds make shadow patterns on some far away hills.

Rex lay back in some heather and closed his eyes. My eyelids were drooping but it was a chance to try a quick watercolour while Frank read to us the first chapters of 'The 39 Steps,' which he apologised again for not having done the previous evening.

'Look, you don't have to do this, you know' He must have been feeling tired too after the unaccustomed exercise but 'No problem' he'd replied opening the well worn copy but not before extracting a pipe, matches and tin of tobacco from his rucksack. 'Keeps away the mosquitoes' he explained but I think it was to get himself 'in character'.

I did a quick sketch of the two of them. Frank read well, puffing away at his pipe, and despite myself I found

I was getting thoroughly hooked on the yarn. He was right. The story bore little resemblance to the films – no 'Mr Memory' at the Music Hall, no nanny, no love interest.

I looked at Rex, whose urban pallor was turning pink. Was he thinking of Guinevere, Hereward the Wake and assembling the cast for his opera or wondering what the FTSE index was today.

Something moved, slithered over a nearby rock and vanished into a crevice.

'My God, I've just seen a snake!' I yelled 'I'm sure it was an adder.'

'Well don't touch it and it won't harm you' Frank advised. I had no intention of going anywhere near it, let alone touching it. I packed up my painting gear and Frank put away his book and nudged Rex who woke up. 'Where am I?' he cried piteously.

As we cleared up, I spotted a small piece of paper taped to the base of the fruitcake tin and handed it to Frank.

'Message from Mother – address of an old school friend of hers who lives in the area. 'She'd love to see you' he read. We all groaned.

Perhaps due to the even lighter load of his rucksack Frank suddenly became a toddler, like Livvie, and as we pressed on down the track, he shed inhibitions and turned into a steam train, lumbering along, chuffing happily and every now and again hooting. A couple of elderly hikers passed us quickly, careful to make no eye contact.

By the time we reached Loch Skerrow Halt, we'd all

developed funny walks. Frank's prancing had slowed down to a shambling gait, Rex looked as if he was walking on coals of fire and I was trying to walk on my toes. Our boots were killing us. The sight of the cool, dark loch was irresistible. We perched on a large rock, having made sure it was snake free and dunked our bare, blistered feet in the icy water. I swear I heard them go 'Hisss.'

Frank produced a small bottle of brandy from an inner pocket and we congratulated overselves on the distance we'd travelled.

'Go-on' I said 'how many miles d'you think we've done. I'd say six.'

'I reckon…. about 7.85' Frank being pedantic.

'Rubbish – must be at least 12' Rex said.

While we enjoyed a brandy and toasted our general fitness, Frank even mentioning next year's London Marathon, I sprang a surprise. Jane and Livvie had given me a pedometer as a little present before they'd left for Canada and I produced it with a flourish from my belt where it had been clipped and studied it carefully.

'Just under four.'

Rex grew angry 'Here, let me see. The thing must be broken.' He snatched the pedometer and hurled it into the loch as if it was a rattlesnake.

'Here, hang on a minute' Frank said in protest. I think I shouted something like 'I just don't believe this' before plunging into the water, accidentally knocking 3 boots off the rock as I did so. Fortunately, two of them were Rex's and one my own.

'Sorry…. sorry….' Rex said as we all groped around

in the pebbles. I just wondered if he was still harbouring a grudge against me for the loss of his mobile and lost opportunities with Alice Van Wotsit. 'I don't know what came over me – put it down to a touch of the sun.' He found it and dried it ceremoniously with his handkerchief off his head. 'Should be alright, these things are usually waterproof.'

There was an uneasy truce, whether it was due to this incident and the possibility that he wouldn't trust me not to shove him over the viaduct on our way back or genuine vertigo I couldn't say but he said shortly afterwards, 'I've got a problem with that bridge thing. There's no way I can face it again.'

We thought about this as we tried unsuccessfully to ease our sore feet back into our boots and it was like trying to squash 6 boiled lobsters into half a dozen eggcups.

'Look, no hassle' Frank gave up on his boots and strung them round his neck, 'why don't you,' looking at me 'make your way back to the car and we'll press on to old Mossdale Station and you can pick us up there. Rex looked incredibly relieved and this plan would suit me too. I'd be able to dash off a quick sketch of the viaduct.

So they hobbled off one way and I hobbled off the other, retracing my steps, shouting cheerily to each other 'watch out for adders' and 'how about giving me the car key' and when we were almost out of ear shot 'D'you want the map?'

I completed quite a spirited pen and wash sketch and felt unaccountably pleased to see the faithful old Morris waiting patiently by the roadside.

On the way to Mossdale, I spotted an old pub, the Grannoch, lying just off the road sheltered by trees. Someone was fishing from a nearby bridge and a young woman with head thrown back and eyes closed was holding a drink. The scene was so peaceful I stopped the car. We'd spend the night here. 'Might be able to take us for just 2 days at a pinch' the landlord said somewhat grudgingly and I expected him to change his mind altogether when I turned up later with two dropouts. But to his credit he didn't and so we came to the end of day one and our first foray into the unknown... and if this sounds like the rounding off of a television travel docu., something the landlord, Duncan, said as he pulled our beer and became more chatty had sparked off this line of thought.

'They're going to be making a T.V. film here shortly.'

'What, here in this pub?' I looked around at it with renewed interest.

'No, no. The area, ye ken. Famous people bin here in these parts. T.V. just think of it' he was impressed by the thought. 'Olympia T.V.' Perhaps I should fix up an ensuite or two.'

What was it? Some memory like flotsam ebbed and flowed on the tide at the back of my mind, finally receding altogether but it left a sinister undercurrent – a nagging worry that stayed with me and wouldn't go away.

SEVEN

With just a picnic lunch under our belts, we fell ravenously upon the steak and chips provided by Duncan, who seemed inclined to talk now we wore shoes and clean shirts.

'So what's this T.V. film about then?' Frank asked just to make conversation.

'Och – it's aboot Dorothy Sayers – the Crime Writer' –

'Five Red Herrings?' Frank broke in.

'That's right. She set it hearaboots. She used to come up and stay at The Anwoth Hotel at Gatehouse – had a partiality for their potato cakes. An' it's aboot other writers connected wi' Galloway... Robert Louis Stevenson, Rabbie Burns, of course, S. R. Crocket.....'

'John Buchan' Frank said excitedly.

After supper, the two of them went into a huddle. It seemed Duncan was of a literary turn of mind and business was not brisk that evening.

I settled myself in a corner and polished up my

sketches while listening to Rex chat up 'Flora' the woman I'd seen sitting outside earlier. She was a fashion journalist, wearing, of course, the obligatory black trousers, relieved by crisp white shirt and seemed as out of place at the Grannoch as I knew Rex felt. He was on home ground here and started off in City Slicker mode.... 'Do you go to Covent Garden?' hoping, no doubt, to impress her with his forthcoming magnum opus.

'Yes – we did a fashion shoot there. We used the scenery for that Japanese thing as a backdrop. It was fantastic.' Not quite what Rex was hoping for but he persevered and eventually struck gold. They had a common interest in very old movies – black and white, of course and were soon discussing 'The Wicked Lady,' 'The Man in Grey' ('that James Mason, he was really cool') and after comparing the rival attractions of Margaret Lockwood and Patricia Roc were about to go on to Humphrey Bogart versus James Cagney when Flora changed key 'Hi Tim, this is Rex. How did you get on?' and to Rex 'Tim likes to fish – all hours of the day or night. He never catches anything, do you sweetie?' I'd seen Tim fishing from the bridge and no wonder he looked so thunderous now if he'd been there all this time without anything to show for it. The couple vanished leaving Rex looking flushed but of course it may have been acute sunburn.

* * *

I'd never played golf before but after a breakfast of porridge and kippers, I felt ready to take up Frank's challenge on the New Galloway 9 hole course. 'Dunc recommended it. Visitor friendly and magnificent views.' I wondered if Duncan would be making up the four but it was just going to be the three of us and we'd have to be discreet about sharing out the clubs apparently as 'Three didn't have any standing.' So, shifty and humble, we paid our fee and attempted to drive our balls up to the first hole. Trying to keep my eye on the ball, as Frank instructed, I thwacked first the ground, then the air, then finally made contact but instead of sailing perpendicular up to the marker, the ball unaccountably veered off to the side, travelling just a few metres. I hacked at it again… and again. Frank was on the skyline snacking on his secrete hoard of survival rations. He beckoned impatiently. Rex, who had also never played before, had driven off with an annoyingly strong and accurate shot and was out of sight. I picked up my golf ball – I examined it for faults – and followed them up the hill. I turned round at the top and was transfixed by the view spread out all around – a panorama of blue distant hills, fertile pastures, moorland and small woods with Loch Ken, a tree fringed strip of silver water, in the foreground, a bridge and, partially hidden, the ruins of a huge sandstone castle. The names of the holes on the golf card were enticing – the 'de'il's ain,' 'hole in wa',' 'Spion Kop' but to me, the scene in front was even more so.

'You go on' I shouted and waved my paint box at Frank, who shrugged his shoulders, nodded and with relief I'm sure, turned to follow Rex. I found the best vantage point and settled myself, leaning against a tree, which I hoped was out of range of wild shots and spent an enjoyable but frustrating hour trying to put down on paper the view with its shifting light and shadows. How can it be so difficult?

We met up later and had lunch in the tiny Royal Burgh of New Galloway. Rex's golf had not lived up to its brilliant start. He put this down to toothache. 'Yeah' I thought. This was also his excuse for not joining us that afternoon on an expedition to Threave Castle, saying he'd sit quietly over a coffee in Castle Douglas but turning down Frank's offer to drive him straight to a dentist. We dropped him off at the main street in the market town and raising his arm as farewell, he hurried off to mingle with shoppers and sparse traffic for a spot of urban renewal.

One of the highlights of our holiday as far as Frank was concerned was to be a sentimental journey across the nearby River Dee to Threave– the stronghold of Archibald the Grim. Great name. Set on an island, the massive grey stone tower looked gaunt and forbidding in reality but softened in the reflection of the weed-strewn river. We had parked the car and walked to a point on the riverbank where a couple and their two young children were waiting, having just rung a bell. Presently, the custodian came to fetch us all in his little boat and so arrived as many must have done through the ages – not with savage intent now but in peace.

Frank wandered off by himself on a nostalgia trip after offering me a toffee and I walked up the steps into the 14th century residence of the powerful despots – the Black Douglases and found myself on the first floor. Below was the dungeon. Misery? Gloom? It had it in spades. I saw the dark shape of a prisoner. Was it a trick of the eye or a shadow? Whatever, it was depressing and I hurriedly climbed the spiral stair to the Great Hall, which was open to the sky. I managed a quick pen and ink sketch of the grand fireplace before the bag of toffees was shoved under my nose again.

We were due to meet Rex at the hotel in the main street and found him in a corner of the lounge behind a table on which were two coffee pots, cup and saucer and, what was this? A folded newspaper! So that was his little game, after all we'd agreed. He saw the direction of my eyes. 'The hotel's' he said. Hmmm. So he said. He'd obviously read it and what else had he been up to? Searching for cyber cafes… fax facilities, a chat in a virtual pub? He sat back and closed his eyes. He looked sort of ill, sick at heart. His was not the face of someone on a carefree holiday. I felt a moment's guilt – his toothache must be worse than we'd thought.

'Look, you really ought to go and see someone about that tooth' I said.

'No, it's passing off.'

We ordered some more coffee, then wandered out to buy plasters for our heels, toes and Frank's eyebrow where he'd been bitten by an insect. We bought postcards of Galloway cattle and bagpipes. 'If sir will allow us to *send* postcards' Rex said sneeringly and Frank picked up some local tourist information leaflets. We looked with curiosity in the window of an Estate Agent, which we passed.

'Good God. I could buy that huge place with 30 acres and have enough left over for that one as well if I sold up in London' Frank said.

I could as well – a tempting thought.

Later, while waiting to order at the 'Chop Chop' (open all hours) Chinese, we studied the further attractions of the area. Mountain biking? No way. Sailing? Maybe. Water sports, gorge scrambling, horse riding? All this sounded a bit too energetic. Rex, being a Foodie – and a picky one – fancied a trawl around local restaurants, harbour side pubs, country house hotels etc. 'Solway scallops, served with a piquant chilli sauce with balsamic vinegar and a touch of black pepper and all that stuff.

Frank felt we should be opting for more simple pleasures, such as bird watching, loch fishing and 'we could sit on a beach. I used to collect shells and paddle in the rock pools' he reminisced. Rex said he'd gone beyond all that.

I liked the sound of Kirkcudbright, inspiration for artists, apparently, with its special light and beautiful scenery round the harbour. I certainly felt in need of some inspiration. I wanted to try a dark, stronger style with a ruined Abbey or a tower house in the foreground.

There was an aquarium next to our table, well lit with water plants waving gently among rocks and a sunken galleon round which a couple of angel fish darted. It was soporific – like the service at 'The Chop Chop.' I had begun to think again that the three of us were completely incompatible and had thought of saying so but the sight of one larger fish making a stately progress round and round the top of the tank with apparently no effort, had a strangely calming effect on all of us and we fell silent watching it – mesmerised. The curious sideways list and dreamy, far away look in its eye held us spellbound.

Then someone appeared to take our order. A comprehensive menu but we steered clear of fish.

I thought Frank might have needed some high tea or supper later on but even he said the thirteen courses had put him on for a bit and sprawled out on an old leather chair at the Grannoch – so relaxed that he left his golf clubs out in the car that night, so relaxed that he forgot to read to us. He fell asleep.

Rex wasn't about to try any seduction technique on two young farmers grumbling about the drought. He closed his eyes and I closed mine. Too much fresh air.

Later, over some drinks I tried reworking my sketch of the Castle I'd made from the golf course. Duncan, polishing some glasses, looked over my shoulder and cast a critical eye over my effort. 'It's no bad.' He put a name to it… 'Kenmure. Home of the Gordon family for hundreds of years. Mary, Queen of the Scots stayed there – her husband, Bothwell, had an estate hereabouts. A grand place but a sad ruin now. Demolition job y' might say.'

'Cromwell?' I asked sympathetically.

He shook his head sadly. 'They just took the roof off last century for tax purposes. Mouldering away noo. No sense of history.'

'Aye' I said 'but it makes a bonnie subject for us poor struggling artists, ye ken.' But he didn't reply.

We wondered what to do the next day if the farmers had their way and it rained. Frank came up with the idea of visiting a 'Walking Stick Museum' he remembered. Well, that would be something different. After that, he was stumped. Rex thought it would be a good opportunity for some serious wining and dining.

The Chinese food had been very salty – it had given us a thirst. After a few more beers, Frank suddenly gave a loud laugh. 'When did we last play 'P.K'?'

'School' said Rex.

A childish game. 'P.K.,' consisting of listing all the reasons why Price-Kettle was such a toadying creep. I recalled a memorable occasion when Rex had got as far as 27.

'P.K's a bastard because he's a two-faced sponger' I started off with the familiar incantation.

'P.K's a bastard because he's a two faced sponger and a puffed up little oik'…..

'A two faced sponger, a puffed up little oik and he interrupts peoples' stories.'

We got as far as 17 without repeating ourselves and we weren't really trying.

We'd once attempted a variation on this game. The new idea was to number his good points but it never really got started – we couldn't think of one. Rex had wondered if he was kind to animals but I'd seen him kick his own dog at Sports Day once. Then I'd put forward the possibility that he was good to elderly people – hadn't there been an Uncle Bart? 'Wealthy, blatantly admitted hopes of legacy' Frank had told us.

We had a nightcap and turned in reasonably early.

I'd been having a dream about Kenmure Castle and kept hearing Duncan's voice 'Demolition job, demolition job!' when I was suddenly, terrifyingly jerked out of my sleep by what sounded like an avalanche of falling masonry. Like a laser beam piercing my brain, the words 'St Ethels – without – the – walls' shot through me. I snapped on the light and looked at my watch to check the date. My God, it was Sunday, the weekend and the City Church was to be demolished. I personally had given the go-ahead but had the consent come through? I hadn't checked. The job would be halfway through by now. Finished by tomorrow. There'd even been a protest march to save St Ethels – an ancient name for a Victorian monstrosity. A last ditch chance of redemption.

The local authority offices would be closed – I couldn't get in touch with anyone.

I couldn't imagine the fine that would be imposed on my practice and there wasn't a thing I could do about the situation.

I found a pen and scrap of paper and made wild calculation. There'd be a legal dispute. The builders would be waiting to start on the block of flats to go up on the site – *that* would have to be put on hold. I looked at my sums, screwed up the piece of paper and started again. Then again. The figures grew too frightening.

EIGHT

Sun streamed in through the windows. Duncan apologised while we had breakfast 'Hope I didn'a wake you. Dropped a crate of empties while I was cleaning up last night.'

'No, no' we said.

I had half a piece of toast – I just wasn't hungry and I snapped at Rex when he suggested my loss of appetite could be due to missing Jane, though he put it in a slightly more crude way.

'Well, who got out of bed the wrong side, then?' he said.

'Well, what shall we do today?' Frank was jollying us up. We didn't reply, I couldn't get my head round any thoughts of pleasure.

'Look, I've got an idea. This old friend of my Ma's. Tattie Shepley-Hepburn.

Rex groaned.

'I know, I know.. but we could just look in for 5

minutes. She's probably a lonely old soul and I know Ma would appreciate it… and we are using her car.

Ah, a touch of emotional blackmail.

'I've looked it up on the map. 'Auchenenoch' we could combine it with a glimpse of Kirkcudbright.'

All right, I was sold. Rex shrugged.

'We might find a nice little eatery there' Frank trying to sell the idea to Rex.

'Well, I'll 'phone her – just a quick drink there – half a hour at the most, promise.'

We couldn't help overhearing. The 'phone was in the bar and Frank didn't know how to talk quietly.

'Hello – it's Frank Hummell – Francis – Barbara Patterson's son. Yes, that's right… Buffy' this last was spoken by Frank doing his impression of someone speaking quietly.

'How are you?' normal voice again. 'Yes, she's in great form. I'm staying nearby for a day or two and I wondered if I could just come and say 'Hello'..... just five minutes…. Well, I've got a couple of friends with me…. Oh no, we couldn't possibly… no really perhaps just a quick drink. Terribly kind of you.' He tried, he really tried but he was weakening.

'Are you really sure? About 12 o'clock? That'll be lovely. Yes, as you say, so much to catch up on. Please don't go to any trouble. Bread and cheese will be fine'…. A hearty laugh. 'Wonderful…. Yes, bye sie.'

'Well, Buffy – how now?' Rex asked with a cruel laugh.

'Sounded as if there was a bloody party going on. The noise!'

So much for the lonely old soul.

'She was keen for us to come right over. At least you can thank me for a free morning' But we didn't thank him. I wasn't feeling magnanimous – the threat of law suits, mega trouble hung over me. The thought of Kirkcudbright now had little appeal,… a visit to an old school friend of Frank's mother far, far less.

'Sunday lunch – might be haute cuisine' he was ever optimistic – but Rex wasn't having any.

'You insisted on bread and cheese remember.'

Frank had visited Auchenenoch once, briefly, as a child and there it was, marked on the Ordnance Survey map so we shouldn't have difficulty finding it.

We'd been comfy at the Grannoch but we had to move on. Duncan had a fishing party coming that evening. We promised to look in again for a drink sometime.

'See ye do,' he said.

I wish I'd been in a better mood to appreciate Kirkcudbright. It would have been no good confiding in the others – Frank's heartiness would grate and Rex would be sarcastic or at best would offer me a cigarette. I didn't smoke, and Rex's habit was beginning to irritate. I had smoked once and it was a reminder of what I was missing. I wished I could have talked my worries through with Jane. As we parked the car in Kirkcudbright, I saw a couple whisk their baby out of its car seat and pop it in its buggy and I had a violent attack of homesickness.

The little town was full of attractions, dominated by another ruined Castle, and with handsome houses and views over the estuary and harbour. Normally I would have sprinted off to look at the harbour, gallery or the homes of two artists who'd lived there – Jessie M. King and A. E. Hornel – one of the Glasgow boys, who sound perennially youthful – those Peter Pans of painters. Today I just trudged sullenly to a bench, sat and stared moodily at the lively and sunny scene and got out my sketchbook and paints.

Rex went off to get his ration of caffeine and Frank had spotted a second hand bookshop.

A few people paused to have a look while I worked. I sensed them but took no notice and they passed on without comment. It must have been about an hour later when Frank slapped me on the shoulder. 'How's it going? Found this.' He waved a copy of 'Five Red Herrings.' 'Dorothy Sayers used to…. Good God – what's going on here?' He took at look at my watercolour and looked up at the pleasant sunny scene, then down again to check. I dipped my brush in the black puddle of paint on my palette and took another swipe at the paper.

'Is that really how you see it?' His tone was sombre. 'Put it away for Heaven's sake – it has perhaps a…. heroic quality' searching for something kind to say 'but I suddenly feel very low'

I studied my work.

'Look get rid of it.'

Rex joined us and stared at it. 'I don't know much about art' (which was true) 'but that fills me with melancholy. Tear it up – it's having a negative effect on my mood.' He hastily lit a cigarette; Frank reached in a pocket for a mint. Both seriously disturbed.

Perhaps I had something after all. This violent reaction to my little effort cheered me up a bit.

Despite the map, we did lose our way and were late arriving at Auchenenoch estate with its winding drive.

We piled out of the dusty car, a testament to the simple life. I'd abandoned shaving and showering and my T-shirt was white no longer but maybe Frank's old and shabby tweed jacket, which he'd hurriedly put on, would save the day. Also, he produced a bottle of Mouton Rothschild, which he'd bought in Kirkcudbright for our hostess.

A large new Mercedes Benz stood on the drive and the house was huge, Regency with a Victorian addition covered in grey cement and Virginia creeper on to which were tacked little bays, minor porches and out buildings. Altogether the sort of house, which normally I would have warmed to. The panelled front door, with its peeling paint and handsome fanlight stood open and we rang the old-fashioned bell pull. A couple of Labradors came bounding round the house and nearly knocked us over but that was all. Frank tried a smart rap on the door, which brought off some more paint but still no one appeared. We stepped inside into the cool dark hall, our footsteps sounding on the old boards and heard distant voices and the yapping of a dog. This was more promising and we pressed on into the gloom. The noise came from behind a door on the left, slightly open. We'd bunched too closely together in the dark and when Frank shoved the door a bit too hard, we fell into the room.

The chat went on without a break. An elderly woman, holding a drink looked up briefly, then bent down to soothe a fat Pekinese which was choking.

'Tattie!' Luckily, Frank had recognised someone – another woman – middle aged this one and thrust the bottle of Mouton Rothschild at her. This certainly did the trick – she smiled at the bottle and then looked up at Frank. She had bleached hair, in fact she looked as if she'd been briefly dipped in a vat of bleach from head to toe being pale, wrinkled and generally dehydrated. Even her blue eyes were faded but not her personality. She'd been attractive once and acted as if she still was – absolutely the right attitude as her enthusiasm, if directed at you, was infectious.

'Ooooo… prezzie wezzie. How too spoiling!' She popped a cigarette into a holder.

Had we suddenly been whisked back to the 1920s or what? We were in a play by Noel Coward – I'd had a small part in 'Hay Fever' at school and felt familiar with the setting – books, clutter, buttoned leather chairs, photos – people spend quids trying to get the look but never get it right.

'Buffy! Wasn't it, 'Puffy Buffy'?' Oh – I'm being naughty telling secrets out of school. Tell me all about Barbara – how is she?' But she didn't give herself time to find out. Rex produced a light for her cigarette – she gave a little girl laugh. 'Introduce me, Buffy.' Rex was introduced with 2 or 3 words of biography and she said how she admired these clever people who work with money in the City. I was shoved forward and her pale eyes flickered over me briefly. The mention that I was an Architect however caused her some interest. 'We've wet rot in the nursery and a bee colony in one of the attics – I think the ceiling below's about to come down.' She looked at me hopefully, expecting me to offer an immediate inspection of these problems but no way was

I about to dispense advice, being still within Dante's Ring of Hell with my own worries so I just murmured 'Mmmm, bad luck' which was probably not the right response as I was ignored after that.

We were in a library cum morning room. There were French windows leading off into a fern infested conservatory and the whole place seemed to be full of people but wasn't really. There was a man, holding forth, with his back to us, a trail of fragrant cigar smoke coming from an ashtray on the edge of his chair – 2 elderly Aunts of Tattie's from Edinburgh, introduced vaguely as Plum and Flitter, one of whom was now telling the dog, Pong Poo to 'Ruddy well shut up' and a homely looking – and I'm being kind here – young woman who was standing around looking spare.

Tattie put away the wine we'd given her in a cupboard. 'Get some more glasses, Jutta' she said to the aimless one – 'German au pair – hasn't been here long' – this was an aside to Frank 'at least she's willing to cook. Impossible to get help nowadays. They all want to do something with computers. My last cook left to become a laptop dancer in Aberdeen.'

We were given wine glasses and the other two had theirs filled with red wine ('drinkies'), then told to 'Come and meet Gavin our future Member – we all hope!' I was being punished but I didn't particularly mind. Before the presentation of Gavin, however, there was a slight commotion. Battling their way through the thick vegetation of the Conservatory looking like jungle commandos with their guns, came two men and the three of us were forgotten.

NINE

They weren't armed intruders, just Ian and Sandy – Tattie's husband and son, who'd been out for a spot of rough shooting on the estate. They threw their bags down on the floor as if they'd been cavemen and there followed much talk and shouting about pigeons and rabbits. Yet another Labrador bounded in and still being on a high, attacked Pong Poo. Frank actually seemed to be enjoying all this, expressing interest in the shooting plans for the glorious 12th, and joined happily in the general clamour.

The splendid bottle of Mouton Rothschild had been a second thought of Frank's – the first had been an inferior bottle of plonk, which conscience and perhaps the vision of his mother's frown had forced him to exchange for something better.

Without in any way being missed, Rex now slipped out to the car, collected the plonk, returned, opened the cupboard and exchanged the bottles. We took our glasses and joined Pong Poo in a race for the exit through the foliage. I caught Ian's slightly surprised look and gave him a wink.

Plum, or it could have been Flitter, came after her dog on to the lawn where we sat and said, more to herself than anyone else 'Lunch will be ages yet. Ian has to have his whisky and lemonade and a bath, if there's any hot water left after Gavin used it all up this morning.'

It was a quarter past three before we sat down in a formal dining room, of beautiful proportions with oils of highland cattle and the obligatory antlers over the mantelpiece. There were linen table napkins, the silver sparkled, Ian said Grace, Frank's stomach gave a loud rumble and we sat down.

Of course, being nine plus lap dog, the seating plan didn't work very well. I was mildly astonished to find that a place had been laid for me at all. I was put next to Rex with Flitter, Pong Poo on her lap, on my right. Ian was at one head of the table flanked by Plum and at the other end, Tattie had Frank on her left and Gavin on her right and Rex, who'd lit her cigarette was to be honoured by being on Gavin's right.

'Ah, pidgy-widgy!' Tattie said as Jutta staggered in with first one steaming and enormous pot and then another. Stodgey pale dumplings floated around in greasy liquid.

'Jutta's so clever with pigeons.'

'Has she taught them to walk on stilts?' This was Rex and he was starting to get chatty which could be bad news.

Gavin Wallace-Gordon-Cowan swung round to

look briefly at Rex and I saw him properly for the first time. He matched the formality of the room in his light grey suit, sober tie and neat grey hair – his eyes were grey too and steely. He looked cool....cold; perhaps the casserole would warm him up.

Jutta was sitting opposite, sandwiched between Frank and Sandy. She was as leaden as her dumplings but as she was the only female under 60, Rex couldn't resist moving into seduction mode and asked her for the recipe. This involved much shouting across the table and words like 'evaporated milk' and 'peanut butter' were tossed around. Peanut butter?

I didn't have to talk as Flitter was absorbed in feeding titbits to her dog. This suited me. It would have been difficult to speak anyway, being busy extracting small bones from each mouthful. Sandy, the soldier, had the perpetual look of an officer gazing into far distant hills for a sighting of the enemy, while his father made one effort at conversation, reminding Plum of the occasion when a visiting cat had attacked his sporran and then fell silent.

I noticed Gavin played around with his food briefly, then put his knife and fork together, while the rest of us struggled on.

'Ho! No lollipops for you!' Rex again.

He was given the full shaft of ice again but surprisingly it started to melt as Rex was scrutinized and a thin smile appeared. I could see nothing in Rex's appearance to make anyone smile – his usual all black gear was looking crumpled and shoddy.

Tattie gave a nervous laugh. Gavin was her star – he must have all the lines. She gave him some cues.

'Gavin's second cousin, Helen Cunningham-Fiske is related to an uncle of mine. The Perthshire Fiske's isn't it, Gavin? And Buffy'- she turned to Frank- 'Aren't I right in saying your mother had a Wallace connection?' But Frank looked blank and it sounded too like 'The Wallace Collection' for Rex to pass it up and he made a weak crack.

Tattie tried again.

'Gavin, didn't you mention your open-air walk about in Kippford next week is going to be televised?'

'So I believe – Olympia TV special length coverage.'

There it was again. I didn't say anything. Rex said 'Why?'

'Only because Gavin happens to be the great white hope at our by-election in two weeks time – our United Loyalists Party Candidate.

'So, where d'you stand – left or right?' asked Rex.

'Ah – it's never as simple as that, is it? I stand for all that is patriotic.'

'Gavin is sometimes called radical, aren't you? Not that I really understand these things,' Tattie twittered.

'Patriotism.' Rex took a pigeon bone out of his mouth 'It's funny you should say that. I'm writing an opera about it.' (Whoops, he was getting a bit ahead of himself here, I thought.)

'Yes, well, why should Wagner have all the good stories?'

'Strange you should say that – he's my favourite composer.' Gavin looked intense now – the steel had become molten – eyes aglow. 'A great intellect, a towering inspiration. Tell me more.'

'I'm interweaving patriotic legends with historical figures into a grand cycle called "Sequence of Swords"; at the end of Act 2 – an act full of pain and passion – there'll be a very moving trio in A minor, my favourite key, Boadicea, Godiva and King Alfred's daughter Ethel Fleda – on 3 chariots, which are slowly burning.' It all poured out, he was unstoppable. Life and death motifs, metaphors, symbolism.....

He had Gavin's attention and Tattie looked impressed. I caught Frank's eye and he looked at the ceiling. The whole table had fallen silent and still he went on.

Over fresh raspberries, he said he would end his epic towards the end of the 19th century with some of Dickens's characters making up a chorus of wounded soldiers being tended by Florence Nightingale.

'Oh, but you can't finish it in the 19th Century.' Gavin managed to get a word in here. 'I can think of some splendid figures in the 20th, who carried the flag for patriotism and all that it stands for... as indeed do I.'

'I suppose you mean Churchill.'

'No, I was thinking of someone else.'

Was he thinking of himself?

'...someone unafraid to say what every thinking person was thinking.' He launched into a full blown political speech delivered with zeal, advocating strictest policies on immigration, toughest punishments for any crime, discipline, control of funds and so on. Such was his eloquence and the fanatical glare he fixed on us and the hypnotic power of his oratory that I almost cried 'hurrah' as he wound up with 'Look at Singapore!' He brought his fist down on the table, causing the delicate china cups, containing instant coffee, to rattle in their saucers.

Jutta called out 'Ya!'

We'd all been transfixed. Rex was the first to come out of the trance.

'My God... You're a bloody...'

A word hung in the air, gathered momentum and would have downloaded in an explosion if I hadn't given him a sharp kick. We were, after all, guests of Frank's mother's old school friend.

'a bloody epitome of bureaucratic absolutism.' This was something we'd learned at school and referred to Philip II of Spain. We'd enjoyed the phrase and done it to death for a term and Rex was now recycling it.

It took the others a while to work it out – if they ever did. Ian was nodding off and Sandy's eyes, which had momentarily refocused at the table thumping, had returned to the far distant panorama.

Gavin said 'Yes, you could say that.' He sounded pleased. 'And we must never forget that in these beautiful Galloway Hills and owning some of the largest estates as far back as the 1930's, there were loyal supporters for our cause – whose descendants rally round us even now. Not only is my walk about, my rally, going to be televised but an in-depth documentary's going to be filmed delving into past history.'

I wondered if this would do him any favours. Such men are dangerous. It was time to go. It was beyond time to go – it was 5 o'clock.

* * *

TEN

Tattie came with us to the car. 'Byesie – hugs to Barbara.'
There'd been animated ' goodbyes' from everyone – some
still seemed to be surprised to see us there but Frank had
made his mark with Ian, who'd been interested in his gun
and had promised him some shooting and an invitation for
the Glorious Twelfth if he was still up here. Frank was
actually sorry to be leaving.

We piled into the Morris, wound down windows,
yelled our 'thank yous' again, prepared to wave…. But
we didn't move off. The battery was flat – that sickening
silence after a splutter. 'Dead as a Dodo' Frank said
unnecessarily. This was more than awkward as we hadn't
anywhere to spend the night.

Tattie's smile had faded but she did the decent thing.
'Of course, you must spend the night – plenty of room.
We're having some people in for drinkies at about 6 – to
meet Gavin – friends and constituents. Should be great
fun.'

It was Sunday but McPhee, the cowman, who was a 'whiz with anything on wheels,' could be consulted first thing tomorrow morning.

We went back into the hall and the only bright spot as far as I could see was that I'd get to look at more rooms and work out the plan of the house.

We were allotted the old nursery in the North wing – two single beds and a collapsed sofa, probably not much used since Sandy and his twin sister Lulu, now nursing in Peru, had romped there. It smelt damp and this was the height of summer. Yes, Tattie was right – wet rot in the woodwork and were we under the bee colony?

I opened a built in cupboard by the fireplace and out fell two badly wounded action men, a pile of their mildewed clothes and their tank. I hoped the handsome Georgian dolls' house nearby hadn't been affected by rot.

Poking my head up the chimney opening, there was a smell of rotting mushrooms and no sign of light at the top. The chimney had been blocked and that was the most probable cause of the trouble – which news I'd impart to my hostess if I was feeling kind.

Reluctantly I had a shave and found a clean shirt; Rex continued as a scraggy crow and Frank sweated in his tweed jacket. After having said 'Goodbyes' to the others earlier, I felt a sense of déjà vu as we came into the hall and met them again but they appeared not to recognise us, thinking we were early arrivals for the drinks party.

Jutta had swapped her role of cook for that of waitress and was lavish with the wine as people poured in. The talk was not about politics but about the Oban

Ball, the hopeless weather for fishing, someone called Jamie Robb-Dilley going off with his shepherd's wife and reels at Stewartston. A very attractive red-haired girl, Issy, asked me how long I was staying. 'Are you coming to Reels at Stewartston on Saturday?' But Rex, who'd been introduced around as doing 'something terribly clever in the City,' swooped like a carrion crow and I was left accepting what looked like a bit of cold dumpling from a plate offered by Jutta.

I saw Frank laughing loudly across the room, his cheery red face a picture of smiling contentment. He looked at home: I felt miles and miles from home. Trapped here, worried sick about St Ethels ….. and what had happened to our plans for a simple, quiet, relaxing break?

The drawing room was in the Regency wing – south facing and the evening sun was throwing up shadows on white panelling. There were some good oil paintings, some family portraits – one a Raeburn – and the soft faded colours of curtains and covers gave the room the look that people spend quids trying to achieve but never do.

I hadn't skulked since my teens but I'd lost none of my old skills and I took out my sketch pad and paint box, settled myself in a corner with my drink and attempted to catch that particular quality of light streaming in and the reflections in the gilt frame mirrors. A hard task, although using white wine instead of water gave my effort a certain splashy je ne sais quoi. I was undisturbed except by Jutta who, seeing what I was doing, gave me a spare glass, which she filled frequently with white wine.

Later on, the charismatic Gavin said a few words to the effect that 'Democracy is dangerous.' His spellbound audience fell silent for a few minutes before bursting into cheers and claps, then the babble continued. I heard someone shout at Rex 'You must be related to the King – Maxwells of Strayne' and I didn't hear him deny it, his arm was round the redhead. He caught my eye, raised his glass, grinning and toasted me.

The party broke up late and supper was a potluck affair in the kitchen, including more left overs from lunch.

We found our way up to the nursery. I flopped on to the old sofa, its bumps, bulges and knobbly springs taking me into its bosom, and fell sound asleep.

* * *

It was late when I woke up next morning. I couldn't bear to open my eyes at first – it felt as if cymbals were crashing inside my head but it was just Frank snoring gently. There was no sign of Rex. Keeping my aching head as still as possible, I dressed and went down. I was desperate to make the 'phone call.

I crept outside, thinking the reception might be better out in the open and tapped the number – no go – a big fat nothing. I'd have to use the 'phone in the house. I saw Rex coming out wearing his fashion shades, clutching a mug in one hand. He looked shifty. We looked at each other. In his other hand he had his mobile. It wasn't a good moment to have a row but I wasn't about to let him get away with it. 'You shifty sod!' I shouted then clutched my head. 'Get wise' he sneered 'you surely didn't imagine I only had the one mobile. Anyway – what about you?'

'It's different for me – I'm a family man.'

He laughed, then groaned.

I still felt too fragile for further recriminations and went back into the house.

Leaving a coin beside the telephone, I tried my office number. Suddenly birds sang, my headache shifted to a minor key, almost vanishing. The consent notice for the demolition had come in the weekend's post so everything was all right.

I went into the kitchen whistling. Why shouldn't Rex have his mobile if he wanted, poor devil. In his sad life of trying to pick up women, his boring job, his opera writing delusions, he needed a bit of pleasure. Ok if it made him happy. I tried smiling as he came in but it seemed to make him uneasy and the whistling was like a pneumatic drill, he complained.

Frank appeared looking pale. We none of us felt like having any breakfast – which was just as well as none was in evidence.

Somehow, McPhee, the cowman, had been alerted to our problem, had gone to fetch a new battery and had popped it in, while admiring our car. I gave him something for his trouble 'Och, it's nothing' he said. 'Watch the fan belt, it looks a wee bit dodgy and you'll need to keep an eye on the water level this weather. Going to be another scorcher.'

Tattie floated into the kitchen in a silk dressing gown, looking a shadow of even her former faded self but she rallied enough to ask 'Fond of reeling?', looking us up and down critically. I don't think she was referring to our uncertain gait but none of us answered. Not encouraged, she went on 'Reels at Stewartston on Saturday, always tremendous fun. We dance in their old chapel – special dispensation from the Pope.' She surely didn't think we'd want to go partying with them – ha bloody ha! But I was feeling benevolent and I smiled.

We said goodbyes again.

'Bysie' I shouted.

I was getting into the car still feeling bullish, when I remembered the wet rot and returned to give Tattie the benefit of a bit of professional advice as a thanks. 'I'll only be two minutes' I told the others. She was nowhere to be seen but I heard voices coming from the morning room.

'Hair of the dog, my dear. I've got something rather special put away and we can enjoy a little drinkie,' Tattie was saying.

'That sounds an excellent idea' – it was Gavin. I heard her open the cupboard and fled before she made a bewildering discovery.

ELEVEN

We were off and it was good to taste freedom again. We were booked in to a bed and breakfast near Creetown, so no worries there, and we planned to spend the rest of the day on a beach doing absolutely nothing. 'I'd like to see Dirk Hattrick's cave, though,' Frank said.

It was noon and the weather was getting hotter by the minute. We stopped to get some petrol at an out of the way service station. There was some road resurfacing going on nearby with that strong smell of melting asphalt hanging in the air. Despite guilty feelings about Tattie's wine and wet rot, gentle waves of relief were still washing over me and I put my head back as Frank made to get out of the car. Through half closed eyes, I saw a large van, with an impressive looking logo, draw up alongside. A series of red arrows dominated an outline of Britain, pointing every which way and the words 'Olympia Television... Always O.T. NEVER O.T.T.'

'Olympia television...' Oh God! And there, getting

out of the passenger seat on the far side with his bottle blonde hair shining in the sun, was Ben Price-Kettle. He hadn't noticed us yet, but soon would with his all seeing eye. I alerted the others – there was no room to duck down in the car: even then I remembered something I'd learned in school Cadet Corp. If you want to vanish, stay put… merge with surroundings. The road mending going on made a quick getaway impossible. We had to think on our feet to save our trip otherwise we might as well go home and none of us had anything to go home for at the moment.

Quick as lightening, I flung a plaid rug over Frank's hair and round his shoulders and instantly he was a bonny, auld woman in her auld car going home to cook lunch for her auld man. I spied an overall hanging by a petrol pump which Rex with a few stealthy movements grasped and donned and, popping on my despised sun hat, made himself useful by polishing the car windows, petrol pumps and anything else lying around, with one of my old hankies.

I became a navvy, spreading grit from the side of the road over my face, giving myself a beer belly with Frank's plus-fours stuffed up my T shirt and ambling with a sideways gait caused by the bulk of these trousers shifting to the right. I had in my hand a very warm can of bitter, which we kept in the car for emergencies and I now proffered this to three blokes, who looked surprised but gratified and thoughtfully averted their gaze from my protuberance.

We talked of this and that – I learned that this very hot dry weather was also not good for mending roads (as well as farming and fishing). At the same time I was trying to keep an eye on Ben. The driver of the van filled up with petrol, while I admired the tar boiler and patted the powered roller, stroking it in a proprietorial way. I watched Ben stretch himself then walk to have a chat with the service station staff – in this case one bad tempered looking man. I wanted to know what he was saying – knowledge is power, they say. I jerked my head at Rex two or three times and eventually he got the message and started polishing the handle of a cupboard near enough for him to eavesdrop. Frank was still slumped over his car wheel as if asleep. I picked up a shovel and admired it, complimented my new mates on the quality of their grit and saw Ben speaking into his mobile. A couple more jerks of my head encouraged Rex, now bending low, to buff up a can of oil lying conveniently near the van.

I took up a rake and dragged it across the road's surface while the can of hot beer was handed round, but I was now becoming aware of raised brows and shrugged shoulders.

'Well cheers!' I said as soon as the van had negotiated the bollards and scorched off out of sight.

Back to our car. The bad tempered guy watched as Rex ceased his compulsive cleaning, flung off overall and hat, Frank put aside his plaid and ruffled his short, thick hair and I extracted the plus fours.

He didn't like what he saw.

'You takin the micky, son?'

'Absolutely not,' Frank tried to reassure him and filled up with petrol quickly. We paid and drove off and heard him hiss 'Sassenachs'; not too loudly but loud enough.

'Which way?' Frank asked us. We didn't want to follow the van.

'Just pull in a minute. Tell us all,' I said to Rex.

'You won't believe this but he was asking the way to Creetown and then phoned Mrs Carnegie to book up for tonight.'

'That's *our* place. The bastard got both addresses from my ma-in-law and he's stalking us.' I was furious. 'We'll have to 'phone her right away and cancel.'

'She's not going to like that.'

'You can say we've been held up or something.'

'You or me?'

I noticed the pained expression on Frank's face as Rex and I both produced our mobiles.

The line was not clear but I managed to get the message through and Mrs Carnegie *didn't* like it. She told me she'd just this minute had to turn someone down. Ben. Oh God! This altered the situation.

'I sent him off to my friend Liz Neilly away over beyond Newton Stewart and I advise *you* to try there next time,' she said abruptly.

'Just a minute, Mrs Carnegie…. We've been held up in a huge traffic jam – haven't moved for hours and I thought it fairer to phone you and cancel but ….. hey… hang on; I think we're starting to move again….. Yes, thank goodness we are! It's a bad line, isn't it? Should see you as we arranged. Bye.'

'What was all that about?'

'Mrs C has no vacancies. Sent Ben off to Newton Stewart ergo we can stay put if we do a bunk right after breakfast. Newton Stewart, if I'm correct, is quite a few miles from Creetown and if he comes looking for us tomorrow, we'll be off on our travels again.' But I didn't like this feeling of being hounded. Why should we be messed around like this?

He was a pain. We discussed it. His media jobs must have culminated in a position at Olympia T.V. via Laurel Rhodes, the presenter we'd seen him romancing in Bar None, and knowing we were going to be in Galloway, had he conjured up projects to cover the area at the same time? Nothing would surprise me. Did he actually think we'd be pleased to have him along? How thick skinned can you get?

Well, he wasn't going to have his wicked way, we'd see to that.

'What if he phones this evening and still wants to join us?' Frank asked.

'We'll arrive late for one thing,' Rex said, 'and we'll be economical with the truth. Say he's a fire risk, heavy smoker, scented candles, leaves electrical appliances on...' Rex was enjoying a spot of creativity.

'Let's forget about him – where's the nearest beach and is anybody hungry?' Frank asked.

We found ourselves in Gatehouse of Fleet again and bought meat pies, crisps, pastries and cool drinks and headed for the nearest beach. There was some sand, not too many people and some shady trees. I promised myself to bring Jane here one day: I could see Livvie tottering around with bucket and spade.

It was a long time since we'd had any food and the pies tasted good. We lounged and even goofed around for a bit, building a dam and Frank joined some kids playing 'pig in the middle.'

I was glad of my hat, the sun was fierce and I mentioned to Rex that he should get a 'panama.'

He jumped up as if he'd been stung 'What did you say?'

'I said you should wear a panama, or a black baseball cap unless you want to come out in blisters.'

'I don't want to hear about it,' he said angrily and strode off down the beach. How sensitive can you get about headgear? But I was feeling mildly euphoric and let it go.

'Right! Who's coming to explore Dirk Hattrick's cave?' Frank asked a bit later 'It's just a bit further along towards Creetown.' He stabbed at the tourist map – now half covered in melted chocolate after a sojourn in his pocket. 'Any takers? You should, you know. Listen.' He now found the place in the tourist leaflet and read out 'This cave derives its name from the smuggler in Sir Walter Scott's book "Guy Mannering"; with its tidal rivers and numerous creeks and bays, the much-indented Solway coastline was ideally suited for contraband trade.' Doesn't that fire your imagination?'

Rex had found a newspaper abandoned on the beach and was immersed in the financial section and just murmured 'Mmm.'

I said 'Would you mind dropping me back at that tower we spotted a little way back…. Grim, gaunt, grey – gouache, I think?'

'Cardoness Castle,' Frank said, consulting his map again. 'Right.' He was only slightly dampened by our lack of enthusiasm for his cave. Rex, in the car now, remained hunched over his paper.

Frank took me to the tower – high on a wooded slope above the road– and drove off.

It was good to be on my own and I concentrated on the stark elevation and the 15th century stonework of its walls, relieved by just a few windows. I slapped on the gouache – being bold with blues, greys, scarlet and lemon yellow. The whole effect was powerful yet uplifting and cheerful. Afterwards, I bought information from the cottage nearby and went to have a look inside the stronghold. The two vaults were covered, grassed over, and a ramp led up to the entrance. The living quarters on the upper floors were reached by a newel stair – the first floor being taken up by the hall. Then on up to the master bedroom and another private chamber with lesser chambers on the 3rd floor and in the attic. For a castle of its age it was surprisingly well provided with mod cons – plenty of latrines, with intra mural vents, all the main living rooms could be heated and the stone bench seats in the window embrasures must have been pleasant places to sit and enjoy the scene through the half glazed windows. From the top there was a dizzying view, (which Rex would have hated) of the lower floors.

They'd been gone a long time. I stood on the ridge overlooking the Water of Fleet and wondered if they'd gone off without me and I wasn't too much bothered by the thought. But no, I heard the familiar and distinctive sound of the Morris engine and there they were – Rex driving.

Dirk Hattrick's cave had not been an unqualified success. It would have been, Frank said, but the approach from the road was steep and wooded and what with scrambling and slipping his way down he was then discouraged by the sight of rocks of all shapes and sizes which would have to be negotiated before climbing into the cave entrance. All this was described in graphic detail. Then he'd come to the cave itself, in the cliff face. It was tight, narrow and he'd got stuck as he went down. 'Thought I'd never squeeze out of the bloody place.' The return journey had been even more treacherous and he'd fallen badly against a rock shaped like a parrot and hurt his leg. He'd crawled and limped his way back to the car, where Rex was asleep, bandaged his leg 'with a bit of old rag' which turned out to be one of my hankies – the one that had done duty as polishing rag at the garage. 'And now, all I want is a stiff drink and a damn good meal.'

* * *

TWELVE

We were feeling quite at home in Gatehouse of Fleet by now and decided to have a blow out at the hotel, where we'd stopped when we'd lost our address on the first night.

'Besides,' Duncan had said, 'Burns had written 'Scot's Wha Hae' there after a day on the moors nearby and where are those sticky plasters we bought for our blisters?' Frank said all this in one breath and applied a bit of first aid to his leg, stopping to point out to us as we drove along... 'That must be the very place where Dorothy L Sayers ate her potato scones!'

We booked a table for dinner and had drinks:- the Burns Room... 'The very room'... Frank was soaking up the area's literary associations like a sponge. 'Where he wrote "Scots Wha Hae".'

A great battle cry – 'Scots Wha Hae.' I tried it out, loudly, and Frank tried it out even louder and it brought the barman in again and *he* explained that they were just the first three words of the opening sentence of a sombre poem, the next three being 'wi' Wallace Bled,' which didn't make much more sense until we strung them together and translated them. Then we got…

'Scots, who have with Wallace bled'… Frank said he must read the whole thing one day when he'd a few weeks to spare.

We all chose the fish for supper and this reminded Frank that he'd brought his rod with him.

'We'll organise a day's fishing first thing tomorrow – with a ghillie and a couple of spare rods and …'

'Hang on, hang on' I said. 'A whole day?' I couldn't imagine it – my fishing experience had been limited to shallow pools and a shrimping net when I was six and I wondered grumpily if Frank would appreciate it if I handed out sketch pads and paints and said I'd planned a day's art for us all. I doubted it.

'You'll love it: A quiet little loch somewhere up in the hills – no sound but the birds and the slap of oars on the water, if we can hire a boat – and you can do some of your painting.'

Thanks! Ok, well, his enthusiasm was halfway infectious and Rex didn't seem to mind one way or the other.

As if on cue, while we ate raspberry trifle, we heard the whine of bagpipes. The lament grew nearer.

'That's Jock Murray – he's practising for the Games,' our waitress said, 'he's really a ghillie but the pipes are very popular with our visitors and he's here most evenings out in the garden.'

'Perfect,' Frank said, and vanished. In a minute or

two there was a sad sound like a monster drawing its last breath, then silence. Then, some minutes later, a wail, some gasps and a high pitched, very loud cry.

'Brilliant.' Frank reappeared 'That's all fixed then. We're meeting Jock here at 9 o'clock plus an extra rod. Just one problem….'

'Which is?'

'The weather.'

'So?'

'Forecast – sunny, cloudless, hot…'

'And?'

'And it's bad news for fishermen everywhere – "fish don't bite if light's too bright"– or something,' he recited. 'Well, I'm definitely up for a challenge. Let's take a nightcap through to the Burns room and plan a wicked picnic.'

We were thinking that we could fry the trout we caught over a small fire 'but perhaps we'd better take along something else – just in case we don't strike lucky,' Frank conceded.

The barman brought us our drinks.

'I'm glad you're still here, sir. There's someone looking for you.'

This was the bloody end! We sat there with furious faces. How the hell had B.P.K. cornered us now?

But he went on 'It's Mungo Douglas and his wife Pat. Locals. They're in the bar. They seem rather annoyed, sir. Apparently something you said about them doing B & B. Well, they don't. Word got around and they've been snowed under with enquiries.'

* * *

We admired the views of sea and gleaming islands glimpsed through trees on the coastal road to Creetown. 'This must be Queen Victoria's favourite scenic route that that couple mentioned,' I said, noticing that Frank didn't flinch now at the name.

We had made a hurried departure from the hotel after settling up. Explanations would have been too complicated. What was it Disraeli used to say? 'Never explain, never complain.'

'I wonder if she liked caravans.' Rex said.

'Only if they were painted dark green.'

'What are you two going on about?' Frank asked 'I was just thinking, I wouldn't mind going to that Reels party Tattie mentioned, on Saturday. Stewartston House, could be fun – a laugh.' I was appalled.

'You can't be serious.' But Rex to my amazement went along with him.

'That gorgeous redhead, Issy something or other, said she was going – yeah could be cool.'

'I'm sorry? I just don't believe this. We haven't been invited, we can't reel and I thought this was meant to be a simple get away from it all break not an excuse for not working and socialising. We have enough of that in the smoke for God's sake.'

'This is different.'

'Oh yes! How different? And what makes you think you can reel – you'd be a laughing stock – it's an art form *and* you've got a gammy leg. You haven't a clue.'

Frank muttered something about – well he could learn, couldn't he…. And it was something he'd always wanted to do.

I was in a sulk after this and we drove up to Mrs Carnegie's semi-bungalow in silence. She greeted us with civility but no great enthusiasm.

No, Mr Price-Kettle hadn't phoned. He'd sounded very nice and she hoped he'd be comfortable at her friend's near Newton Stewart. 'Breakfast is at 8 o'clock' and she showed us to our rooms.

Rex noticed that the telephone was in the hall. 'It's only ten thirty, he still might ring,' he said. Worrying thought. We went to retrieve various things from the car, such as Frank's plus fours – needed, he said, for the fishing trip despite a forecast of 25°C for the next couple of days. 'So, let's see what you made of that Castle today.' He was trying to soothe ruffled feathers now.

I showed him my gouache.

'You know, you're not so bad at buildings, are you? I vaguely remember being shown round the place as a child. Ancient. They used to use moss as loo paper, didn't they?' It was all he remembered of Cardoness.

I noticed Rex hovering in the hall and watched as he deftly unplugged Mrs Carnegie's telephone.

* * *

Frank arrived at breakfast limping heavily, dressed all in tweed and sweating already at 8 am. This didn't deter him from enjoying the full Scottish breakfast. I asked for bacon and toast and made up some sandwiches for myself for lunch, which amused the others. 'No need for that – we'll get something tasty in town,' Frank said.

By the time we'd finished breakfast, paid up and

rattled along at speed (it felt like 80 miles per hour but was, in fact, only about 50), it was 9 o'clock and we could see Jock waiting for us by the hotel entrance, rod in hand, canvas bag on shoulder: he smiled. Frank went to greet him but not before telling Rex to hoof it to the nearest shop and assemble a picnic.

It was a perfect summer's day.

'Och! The weather's nae guid,' Jock grumbled quietly. I hoped someone was enjoying it.

With great difficulty, Rex squashed himself into the back by me and Jock settled himself in the front, giving directions as we left the town and headed up into the hills to Loch Whinyeon.

'Bonny wee car. Mrs Petrie Scott of Daltaggart, the big hoose, used to own one and the only time it ever let her doon was when she tried to run awa' wi one of the McKenna boys.' There was plenty more in this vein on the 15-minute drive.

We pulled up by the side of the road. Apart from a small-whitewashed farmhouse there was no sign of human habitation – no traffic on the narrow road, no sound other than intermittent birdcalls. The moor stretched away up the hill to our right and when we'd organised who was going to carry what, we set off up a rabbit track. Jock, nimble as a rabbit himself, sprinted along despite being, I should say, fifteen or more years older than us and despite the fact that he seemed to be carrying the heaviest load.

Frank very soon got out of breath and sank down into the heather.

'Snakes!' I hissed but he didn't budge.

At the brow of the hill, we looked down to the other

side and there was the loch spread out – blue and tranquil, tiers of low green hills and beyond, in the distance, higher blue Galloway hills. It was a short walk now down to a little wooden hut and a short pier, where a small pale grey rowing boat was tied up.

After making our base camp at the hut, where Jock said, hopefully, we could shelter if it rained, he looked at us critically.

'We'll try some flies first, then if that's nae guid, we'll do some dapping after lunch.' We were going to be there for the day. He nodded his head approvingly at Frank's tweed ensemble. He was wearing tweeds himself but his had grown thin with age. I suppose Rex might resemble a black cloud but I realised that my orange shirt was a no-no when it came to fooling fish.

'If you sit up on yon hill, folks might think ye're one of those Buddhists from the other side of the moor. Did you see that programme on the telly? There're going to do another, I hear.'

'Noo, I can tak twa o' ye.' He clambered aboard one of the dinghies and untied it. There was no holding Frank and the little boat rocked perilously as he stepped in. Rex and I looked at each other. I didn't even know what we were fishing for… salmon? Perch? Tench – was there such a fish?

'I'll toss you for it,' Rex said and produced a coin.

'Heads you win, tails I lose.'

I wasn't thinking.

'It's tails – off you go,' he said and off I went.

* * *

THIRTEEN

Surprisingly, that morning out on the loch was one of the happiest I'd spent in a long time. My cares and problems dissolved as I concentrated on the dry fly at the end of my line skimming the surface of the water and trying to cast with the wrist action demonstrated by Jock. As a calmer, this has no equal. A visit to the gym, yoga, a walk, a good book? Forget it. I wasn't sure if shark fishing or tussling with a huge salmon on a river would have quite the same restful charm but loch fishing combines the brilliant excuse for thorough idleness with the thought that you're doing something undeniably worthwhile – providing food – a basic human need.

It was brown trout we were after and Jock with nimble fingers had tied a fly and hook to each line. I'd never realised what beautiful miniature works of art these flies were. Tiny feathers bound tightly to give the impression of wings. Art imitating nature, it flies through the air and as it lands briefly on the surface of the water, the fish beneath scramble for a tasty morsel. At least that's the idea.

'I mind the time when…' And he was off again, in his soft lowland accent telling of scandalous yarns, local gossip, ghost stories, legends and eccentric characters he'd come across, puffing intermittently on his pipe while the smoke and smell from the baccy mesmerised us.

Now and again, he decided to try a different fly on our lines. Some had cheeky names.

'Try this' he said, picking out a particularly exotic one from the assortment in his tobacco tin and attaching it to Frank's line. 'Queen o' the South.'

'I thought that was a football team' I said.

'Aye, they called the team after the wee fly ma great-grandfither made. I made this one. A wee laddie from London caught a four pounder wi'it just last week.'

Oh yeah? I was sceptical but Frank was excited and cast with renewed enthusiasm. 'I want to feel 'that twitch on the end of the line' as Father Brown said.'

I was offered 'Godzilla' – another of Jock's creations but it was obviously siesta time down under *or*… no, it couldn't be… perish the thought… but could it be that Jock's ceaseless chat was ringing alarm bells through the water?

We rowed near to the only other boat on the loch.

'We'll see if they've found a guid patch' and Jock winked at us as we raised our rods.

The two men were silent and brooding; their scowls deepened as we came near.

'Any luck?' Jock shouted.

'Do you mind' one said in a voice barely audible. So Jock retaliated by much splashing with oars and churning of water.

He took us to the far side of the loch – an even more lonely spot, out of sight now of the pier. No trees, just heather, bracken and dry coarse grass. We heard about the wild goats, an eagle's nest, wild mink and the unlikely ghost of 'Fred,' the Galloway Boar, trotting through windswept hills on nights when the moon was full. Jock closed his eyes, hypnotised by his own monologue, puffing now and then on his ancient pipe which nestled comfortably between the gaps in his teeth.

The silence was suddenly interrupted.

'Look – good God!' Frank stood up, rocking the boat 'I've got a bloody bite!'

'Strike!' Jock yelled and got ready with the net. 'Doon an' up!' but it got away.

'Must have been huge – the pull was terrific' Frank was already fantasising. 'Six pounder?' he asked Jock. 'Aye' he was as disappointed as Frank.

'D'ye ken 'The Five Red Herrings?"' he asked, perhaps hoping to divert us from failure. 'Ma uncle Jack taught the writer to fish' or perhaps it was to re-affirm his credentials as a ghillie.

'Yes, I heard she used to stay up here.' I think Frank was pleased with this literary link – he'd actually been fishing with someone whose uncle had shown Dorothy Sayers how to cast.

'… Or was it John Buchan? Ah weel…' Jock looked at his watch and knocked his pipe on the side of the boat. Frank pre-empted him.

'I could kill a roast beef sandwich. Lashings of horseradish, thick white bread. Or fish and chips – five red herrings even – loads of ketchup.'

We raised our rods and reeled in our lines while Jock rowed us to food and shelter. I'd taken off the offending shirt and now my back was burning.

The talk had dried up but Jock started to whistle softly. First 'Annie Laurie' which led seamlessly into 'My love is like a red, red rose' and then the irritating little signature tune which always preceded 'The News' on Olympia T.V. and which I now realised was a cunning blend of the two. He realised what he was whistling.

'Which reminds me – a wee bit of excitement. We're going to be on the telly 'Country Sports in the Stewartry – an' I've a wee part mysel.' They'll be askin' for ma autograph' and he chuckled.

Frank caught my eye.

'When's this then?'

'Verra soon' was all he knew. He rowed alongside the pier and we scrambled out.

Rex – a disreputable starling – sprang from behind the hut, dusty and smelling of smoke. 'How many?' he asked. He became less chirpy when we gave the thumbs down. 'I had a bite – it would have been a whopper' Frank said mournfully. 'God, you smell like a kipper factory.'

'I'd got everything ready for 'trout au feu'.' Rex took us round the back of the shed where a fire was blazing away. A grate and the grid over it had been improvised by some stones and bits of wire and metal he'd found lying around. He was proud and gazed at it fondly but

Jock was aghast 'Put it oot. Noo!. D'ye want to set the whole moor alight? Good God mon, the whole place is tinder dry – just one spark…' words failed him. It sizzled dismally as we threw loch water on it by means of an old pan and a baler from the boat.

'So who's in charge of the catering, then?' Jock looked at us. 'Don't bother aboot me – I've ma Lockerbie Cheddar sandwiches – I'll be awa over the hill collecting grass hoppers.' Were these a delicacy to go with his sandwiches, I wondered– but no. 'and we'll do some dapping after lunch.' I was none the wiser.

'So, come on' Frank getting desperate now. 'Where's the picnic? What did you get in that shop?'

'Well, it was just a newsagents – you were all in such a hurry… I bought a paper and these…' Rex produced a packet of oatmeal ginger biscuits and a small pot of honey… I was going to crumble the biscuits over the fish, add a bit of honey et voila…. A fish fit for a laird.'

No fire.

No fish.

No food.

Frank looked stupefied. I was feeling surprised. This was about the first creative contribution Rex had made since our trip had started apart from nicking the Mouton Rothschild and he didn't seem at all dashed.

Frank turned his gaze on me. I remembered my bacon sandwiches, derided at breakfast time: I unwrapped them slowly, deliberately and knew his mouth was watering.

'Go on, then.' I offered them round. Frank said they were the best sandwiches he'd tasted in all his life.

They didn't go far but the ginger biscuits and honey were pure nectar and we vowed to try the combination again soon.

We wondered idly if Jock had eaten all his sandwiches. The thought of Lockerbie Cheddar was tantalising.

He picked his way nimbly over heather, stopping now and then to pounce and returned with his jar of grasshoppers.

Frank was going to try dapping and Jock made sure that Rex would be under his surveillance and not lighting any more fires. I stretched out lazily and watched them set out. Dapping seemed to involve gentle jerking of the rod. A light aeroplane flew overhead. Frank had been about to read another chapter of 'the 39 steps' to us when Jock had returned from his grasshopper hunt and I picked up the book. Richard Hannay was running 'like blue lightening' across bare, heather hills like these, looking for cover from his enemies. A monoplane was flying low looking for him. I closed my eyes. The droning of the light aircraft was restful. It was getting louder and I opened one eye, screwing it up against the sun. A flash of silver dazzled: on the underside of each wing was painted a logo in blue. It flew low, circling once then rose and flew eastwards. I saw Jock give it a wave but our attention was diverted as Rex shouted 'Get ready with the net!' and even from where I was sprawled out, I could see he'd caught something large and fish like. Typical!

I sat on the pier and studied the minnows darting below, then yielded to temptation and picked up Rex's newspaper – full of the usual stuff, rape and pillage, coups in foreign parts and triumphant overthrows of coups in foreign parts. On page five, down at the bottom was a small photograph of the remains of St Ethel's – without –the-Walls and a bleak looking cluster of people holding a banner on which was written 'IN THE NAME OF GOD... WHAT NEXT?' well... a development, actually. And we needed more of the same kind if our practice was to survive.

Rex's brown trout was a respectable size and weighed in at 1lb 12oz on Jock's imperial hook scale. Frank looked glum, Rex euphoric as they came ashore. Jock was just finishing a story '... That was why I'd never go out stalking again wi' Sir Hector.' He saw me 'Did ye see Mr Erskine's plane? They say it cost thousands. Well, nae doot he can afford it. Lives over at Glen Stramon – ugly, auld hoose but fine loch. I stocked it for him last year. He's head of some media company. He has a helicopter too.'

The logo on his plane had looked vaguely familiar....

This was all very interesting but I suddenly realised that we hadn't booked anywhere to sleep that night.

Jock recommended asking down at his brother in law's caravan site on the coast. 'He sometimes has one or two he lets out for the night.'

We could have fried the trout on the car bonnet. We thanked Jock, dropped him off and followed his instructions for 'the Old Meikle Holiday Park.'

If the car had felt like an oven, the caravan felt like a furnace. It was the only one available, was meant to sleep just two and smelt like the filthy contents of a laundry bag.

Frank and I looked at each other and shook our heads slightly.

'We'll take it!' Rex said. 'I'll cook my trout for supper. How's that?' He looked at the small gas ring.

'Easy, tiger' I said 'for one thing, this caravan's crap and for another your trout's gone off – couldn't have survived in this heat.'

'I could hang out very happily in here.' Rex protested 'Where's this 'simple life' you're always going on about?' And so we were shamed into spending a night in that hellish inferno, while Rex fried his fish and we bought double portions of cod n' chips.

This new up-beat Rex disturbed me. A jackdaw now with a sparking diamond ring.

The mood swings made me wonder if he was into some substance abuse. Surely the catching of one fish couldn't have lifted him on to such a high…

* * *

FOURTEEN

It was no cooler next day. We'd added an extra layer to the smell with Rex's fish and were glad to settle up and get out. Frank fancied sea breezes to clear the lungs and suggested sailing. There was sailing on Loch Ken, which we'd seen from the golf course. Water-skiing and windsurfing were also offered but Frank was adamant about the sea. I knew there was no way he'd ever be persuaded to try the energetic water sports if a dinghy wasn't available – no – water skiing and windsurfing wouldn't be his line at all, nor mine come to that.

We studied our leaflets.

'Kippford it is,' he said.

'Great!' said Rex, worryingly.

'Well, on one condition,' I said. 'A morning at Sailing School and an afternoon at Dundrennan Abbey. Fair's fair.'

'Definitely up for that!' Rex said.

The roads were empty but the pretty seaside village

of Kippford was seething with activity. We managed to park the car but it meant a long walk back down to the harbour. We sat on a wall and people watched – stunned by the buzz. We hadn't seen so many people gathered together for days and it felt strange.

There were plenty of yachts and dinghies of every size and class, instructions being shouted, ropes coiled or uncoiled, sails being unfurled. Everyone down to the smallest child wearing his life jacket seemed to have a specific purpose in mind. We felt spare and intimidated and Frank suggested we go for a pint. A stalling tactic?

A little pub opposite was crowded too.

'Perhaps we've hit Regatta Day or something.' Frank shouted.

'Can't hear you' I shouted back and I don't think I'd ever said that to him before.

We gave up trying to shout above the din. In the competition for the loudest voices, we lost and the sun tanned, 7 foot Yahoo Yachties won hands down.

Trying to salvage his morning, Frank attempted to strike up some chat and ask about the Sailing School but was mistaken for one of the instructors and gave up after that, not wishing to show crass ignorance in front of these experienced old hands. None of us really cared and we had a let out in the weather. The big complaint today was lack of a good, strong breeze.

'Wouldn't have been much fun. We'll come back when there's a bit of a wind.' Frank said. We were glad to agree – relieved that we wouldn't have to make fools of ourselves on the water. I never did Arthur Ransome.

We stocked up on crisps and sandwiches and found

that outside the pub, there was a new flurry of excitement. A small crowd had gathered – most of it consisting of men dressed in pale grey shirts and trousers and women wearing pale grey T-shirts and trousers. They fluttered around like moths and the bright attraction at the Centre – also in pale grey, standing on a little platform, looked familiar.

'Hello, what's this? It's that bloody Gavin something – hyphenated something, isn't it?'

Apart from his loyal army of supporters, Gavin didn't have many to harangue or convert. We weren't over keen to be recognised but felt again the power of his personality and were drawn closer.

'Tattie mentioned something about a Rally. I suppose this is it.' Frank said. 'Split up and he won't get the connection.'

I didn't think he was looking at the small crowd – he was away in a world of his own. His idyllic world of zero tolerance and world domination.

Soon, like iron filings pulled to a magnet, people drew near from around the harbour. 'The hearties' stopped shouting, ropes were left uncoiled, main braces left unspliced, tins of varnish and paint congealed in the heat.

We'd heard a lot of it before but, dangerously, I found myself joining in claps and cheers, while furious moths descended on one brave heckler, whose emotions hadn't been harangued.

I suddenly noticed a large van behind the platform and I recognised it. The arrows and triangle logo was the same one I'd noticed on the plane yesterday. This rally was being televised by Olympia T.V. and now, coming round the back of the van to talk to the cameraman was Price-Kettle!

Gavin was about to do a walk about and his gimlet eye had suddenly fixed on Rex. He pushed his way arrogantly through the throng, one grey arm raised to silence the mob.

'This loyal supporter and true friend of all of us here today (here he held up Rex's thin arm) has begun an immense undertaking for our cause…

….A patriotic Opera to rival the whole of Wagner's Ring Cycle.'

A moment's silence for this profound announcement to sink in, and then a thunderous roar of applause.

Rex took it all well, smiling modestly – well, if he never gets to write the damn thing, he's had his moment of glory. 'We wish him all success.'

Gavin squeezed his arm, gave his thin regal smile and 'Good to see you here.' Rex opened his mouth as if to say something profound but Gavin passed on and the moment was gone.

Well, one thing was certain, P.K. would never have associated Rex with that build up. Luckily he'd been diverted back into the van but had emerged briefly when he'd heard all the noise to see what the fuss had been about.

I gestured frantically to Frank who waved the car keys at me and started off up the hill.

He had to drive down to the harbour to pick us up and by the time he returned, Gavin had stepped on to a yacht and was acknowledging more cheers. Had he realised that only a very small percentage of these admirers were locals? The others having no rights to vote in the by-election.

I grabbed Rex, who was still one of the crowd and still in a daze from the ovation. I explained the situation and we scrambled into the car. The engine of a Morris Minor has a distinctive sound, at least this one did – rather like a motor boat– and there was a gutsy noise as Frank revved up and we juddered forward in third gear instead of first. Pulling the choke out too far caused it to back fire. At this sound, like a pistol shot, someone screamed.

A murderous attempt on Gavin? 'ASSASSINS MAKE GETAWAY IN MORRIS MINOR.' I could see the headlines.

The commotion had caused Price-Kettle to see what was going on. He looked at the car, frowned then caught my eye. He started waving.

'Come on, come on, faster – he's spotted us. Good God, he's running after us!'

Frank put his foot on the accelerator and we were soon chugging away from the harbour and lost him.

'He knows our car now. He'll recognise it' Frank said.

'But he won't be able to follow us – he doesn't know where we're going and neither do we' I reasoned.

We grazed on the wheel and managed to hit the right road to Dundrennan Abbey, which lay just off the one from Auchencairn to Kirkcudbright. We parked in the sleepy village and I wandered off to enjoy the ruins. Frank didn't do ruins. He said he'd study the map and plan what he called a 'proper walk' for the next day. All things, including our blisters, being equal, he reckoned we could manage about 10 miles. He said we owed him one a) because he'd missed out on his sailing and b) because of that shifty business about the mobiles for which he wanted a full explanation some time – how come we had managed to conjure ours back from that watery grave?

I strolled round the ruins of the ancient Abbey. Only the walls of the transepts, a fine archway and one perfect pointed doorway remained but there was plenty of atmosphere here and I found just the right perspective for a painting – dark again, I planned, but mellow this time.

Rex perched in the shade nearby. Still in his ivory tower, he said the creative juices were flowing, asked to borrow a pencil and commenced the writing of his masterpiece on a cigarette packet.

I don't think two hours have ever gone by so quickly. It was difficult to convey the strength in those proud high walls and the sense of sombre tranquillity – sad because, according to legend and the leaflets, Mary Queen of Scots spent her last night in Scotland here with the monks murmuring prayers for the Queen who shared their faith.

I got up to stretch my legs and saw Frank asleep, propped up against some stones with the map spread out over his head acting as a sun hat, lost to the glories of Medieval Ecclesiastical Architecture.

'Hi, how goes it?' Rex, cigarette in his hand now instead of pencil, was in a happy trance. There was not much room on the packet to write an epic but I could just make out two words... ACT 1. Well, it was a start.

'Ideas coming faster than you can write them?' I asked. He inhaled deeply.

'I see the whole thing as a spiritual journey, using the sea as a metaphor... tempestuous you understand, with a volcanic undertow and violent eruptions from time to time. Music surging, swelling, ebbing.... Isolation.... Independence.

Was this genius or what?

It seemed a bit prosaic to ask how the plot was going to kick off in Scene One after this. Had he *lost* the plot? I just asked 'When does Lady Godiva make her entrance?' but he was miles away – and miles away from fund managing schemes and urban gridlocks too, so that was good. After all that was why we were here – to forget the big, bad world and chill out in this blistering heat.

I was sure the cat and mouse game with Price-Kettle was over. We'd be awa' up in the hills on our 'Big walk' tomorrow and we didn't even know where we'd be staying the night ourselves – which reminded me..........

'Wow – that's fantastic!' Enthusiastic praise for my painting left on the grass. 'I really mean it – brilliant.' She was in her early thirties, I guessed, quite attractive in a pale, sharp way. Ginger hair, black roots. Safari outfit.

'Thanks. I wasn't sure about that touch of purple....'

'It's perfect. Oh – I know it's not oil but I should say very Peploe, you're a real colourist, aren't you?'

I'd tried to get away from my usual architectural style so was pleased by all this, deciding she was a woman of style and discernment.

Rex came out of his trance, stubbed out his cigarette and joined us, no doubt jealous of this sudden attention directed at me. He stared at my painting 'God, yes, super. You must have it framed and give it to Jane for her birthday.' There should be no nonsense here about me being available. He smoothed back his hair and moved in – Rex, the sleek blackbird.

I wondered if he'd start off with vivid descriptions of his putative opera but he tried a different gambit.

'You're from London, aren't you – I can tell.'

Crafty, this. If she said 'Yes' he was off to a flying start and how could he tell etc. and if she said 'No' Edinburgh' well it was some sort of a start and he'd rustle up phantom friends who lived there.

Anyway, it had been a good guess and yes, she was from London, Balham. He was surely about to pin her down further when she looked at her watch, sighed, took out of her pocket a whistle and blew two short blasts and one long one.

From different parts of the Abbey, from behind pillars and posts, appeared four men and another woman all about the same age.

'Any luck?' she shouted. 'We're a team. 'B' team,' she explained to Rex. 'A sort of Treasure Hunt thing today,' and she ran to join the others, so that seemed to be the end of Rex's chances there.

One of the men, bald, red in the face and out of breath from running, flopped down on the grass by us while the others got together in a huddle, like a rugger scrum, then patted each other on the back.

We must have looked surprised so he told us 'In-put

and confidence boosting. Courtney's a born teamster.' He shrugged his shoulders 'Not sure I'm cut out for this. Bit of a maverick.' He smiled 'Corporate bonding's the name of the game.'

I'd heard of this sort of thing and some of Rex's brother companies went in for it. We listened fascinated while he opened up about the terrors of C.B. as he called it, surreptitiously accepting a mint.

His name was Errol and he was with C.R.S. – City Resource and Strategies, recently merged with Development and International Planners Inc (D.I.P.I.)

'Crass – Dippy. I know them' Rex said.

A huge outfit apparently. The amalgamation had caused massive internal reorganisation, pruning, purges, promoting, redundancies, not to mention mega insecurity with jobs vanishing overnight. And as if that weren't bad enough, there was now that feeling that 'Big Brother' was watching all the time.

'Somebody forcing you to stay?' I asked.

'Yeah – me. And why, you ask. Well, it's lonely out there. Pay's good, while it lasts, and maybe a tin handshake at the end of it…. Loyalty bonus.' He closed his eyes and leaned back 'What I really want is to grow a beard and be an archaeologist.'

'Well, you can enjoy old bones and stones as a hobby, can't you?' I asked.

He gave a bitter laugh. 'Hobby? Hobby? You must be joking. Hobbies are definitely out – a big steal of company time, see.'

'Weekends? Evenings?'

He opened his eyes. 'No such thing. Company

devours you – it gobbles up any private life you might have had. Ask anyone. See Con over there.' He indicated a blue shirt 'He has hang ups about his girl friend now. They were planning to tie the knot soon but word reached him on the grape vine that her face doesn't fit. It doesn't say much about his loyalty and devotion to her but you get the picture. And Serena Price-Kettle is a real looker. Not that looks are everything of course....'

At this name, I saw Rex jerk completely out of his trance – and no wonder. Rex and Serena had been an item at one time and I remembered I'd had my suspicions (at the time) that was why Rex had tolerated, even encouraged, her cousin Ben. And this had given Ben the idea that we liked his company – which was rubbish. But back to Serena. Yes, she was stunningly attractive but she was a wild child. Rex would vouch for that – he'd had a miserable time with her. Unless she'd had a conversion, I could see the Company's point of view. She was bad news, definitely.

'You know her?' Errol had seen a glance pass between Rex and me. 'Well, you know what I mean. Actually, she's coming up here this weekend. Her cousin's in television and they're doing a programme on archaeology in the area. There's a lot of it about – a dig going on at the Motte, burial stones near Gatehouse of Fleet, tower houses, ruins like this – you name it. I want to be in on it – it's my thing – instead of playing kindergarten games like this.' He kicked at a pile of rubble.

So Ben P.K. had covered bones and stones too. Was nowhere safe? Thank God we were doing the 'Big Walk' next day.

'You ought to visit Stewartston House' I said, remembering something Tattie had said about a small family museum of curios kept there. 'They've got some mementos of Mary, Queen of Scots.... A lock of Bonnie Prince Charlie's hair.....'

'There are locks of his hair all over the place – no wonder he had to wear a wig. Is the house open to the public?'

'No idea' I said 'There's a party there on Saturday but it's private.'

'Talking of Mary Queen of Scots, though – that's why we're here – we've got these clues but we've come to a full stop.'

'Can I help?' I asked. After explaining that personal initiative i.e. cheating, was frowned on, that they all had to march to the same tune, toe the line etc. he decided it wouldn't do any harm to read it out as if to himself.

'Pillar of society she was not,
In history a turbulent chapter,
Scots still mourn this
Catholic, cloistered
In a castle before death, married to a
Knave. Her life would have been better had she
Altered it.'

'It all points to an Abbey,– pillar, Chapter House, cloister, nave, altar and we've got the Mary Queen of Scots link here.

I looked over his shoulder.

'Piscina' I said. 'First letter of each line. Piscina, obvious.' He looked blank. 'By the altar, a niche scooped out of stone for holy water. By the way, they've spelt nave 'Knave'.

'Never heard of it.'

'Trust me – I'm an architect.'

'Bloody hell – this puts me in an awkward position. Against all the rules. Thanks anyway.'

The rest of his team were scattered. Rex, whose previous high spirits had been subdued by the mention of Serena, lit another cigarette and went to try his luck with Courtney again.

'I'll have to get my head around this.' Errol struggled with his moral dilemma but then there was a shout from 'blue shirt.' He'd found the next clue by accident – no moral problem there as the team hurried to read it. They rushed to their mini bus and were gone. Two minutes of tranquillity and another team arrived.

I gathered up my painting things and saw Rex strolling back looking up beat again.

'They're staying at a hotel near Dalry called 'The Barreough' – two rosettes, Taste of Scotland, not too posh. Not that they're able to indulge. Making their own meal tonight by a campfire on the coast using only natural ingredients. Seaweed stew – no thanks. Anyway, the hotel sounds o.k. Shall I give it a buzz?' He gave me a challenging look at the suggestion of using his mobile but I'd given up the battle.

'Do that.'

We went to find Frank and found him asleep with the map still over his eyes, his jaws chomping on imaginary sweetmeats, just as I'd seen Livvie doing after she'd had her feed and was fast asleep. After prodding him awake, he was keen to top up his energy levels and agreed 'The Barreough' might be just the place to do it.

FIFTEEN

Our drive to Barreough took us along the South side of Loch Ken, through the pretty village of Dalry– full name St. John's Town of Dalry as according to legend, St John the Baptist had sat on a stone at the top of the hill there to admire the view... Well, that's what Frank quoted from one of the guidebooks and we weren't going to argue about it. He also told us we were near Lochinvar loch and did we remember the poem about 'Young Lochinvar,' who came out of the West, from Walter Scott's 'Marmion?' In case we'd forgotten, he refreshed our memories with a recitation.

The hotel was on a hill, with fir plantations as a backdrop and a rushing stream in the foreground. Small, Scottish-Baronial in style, built of pink sandstone. I hoped I might be in one of the fairytale turret rooms at the top.

In fact, I was in a small attic room at the back but after the horrible caravan of the previous night, it was the Ritz.

I put on my one clean (crumpled) shirt – pink – and tartan tie, (bought on impulse in Richmond), after a shower but didn't shave, in deference to the simple life we were supposed to be leading and met the others in the bar. Frank in tweed and Rex, hawk like in black (crumpled) long sleeved shirt.

Rex had heard rumours of a cocktail called Rob Roy, a mixture of whisky and coke and thinking this would be appropriate egged on the barman to give it a whirl.

We all ordered a Rob Roy and tried to muster pleasure as we drank.

The décor at the Barreough was retro-Scottish grannie – chic meets big white hunter, the big white hunter bit being chiefly in the bar and hall where the eyes, set in great deer and tiger heads, gazed far away over our heads to some old remembered stretch of moorland or Indian jungle. Knives and guns, long disused, telling of savage deeds, were now arranged in attractive intricate patterns chiming surprisingly well with chintz and tartan. There were faded photographs in thin gold frames, bowls of flowers and copies of 'The Catering Times' generously distributed on small oak tables.

Of the 'A' team there was no sign, nor of the 'B' team. They were probably down on the shore even now, gathering fruits of the sea and looking forward to a culinary challenge.

We felt we deserved a *digestive* challenge and took it up with a Provencal paté, followed by coq au vin, followed by raspberry parfait. Not exactly a taste of Scotland. A French menu. The Auld Alliance lingered on perhaps. Anyway it was good, better than good.

The dining room (tartan, antlers, baronial fireplace) had been more or less empty until the cheese and coffee. Frank had done his homework and put forward various options for the Big Walk and they were:

The Raiders' Road. This was another of Frank's literary quests with connections to a book called 'The Raiders' – a tale of gypsies, smugglers and cattle thieves. Short amble along road might be ok.

A climb up the Merrick – highest peak in the South of Scotland – (put off by word 'highest' – Wasn't sure we'd be up to it. Also the Merrick Hills are known as 'The Awful Hand'. I didn't like the sound of this).

Glen Trool, scene of Robert the Bruce's victorious battles to gain Scotland's independence. Remembering the story of his encounter with the determined spider I'd heard as a child, I thought I might manage a stroll to the Bruce stone.

Loch Enoch – the highest loch in Britain with silver strands. The name appealed. Was intrigued by 'silver strands.' The word 'highest' though, rang alarm bells again.

'Well?' Frank looked at us.

Rex seemed to shrink down into his black shirt and said nothing.

'How about a stroll along to Bruce's stone' I said 'or what about going to see Annie Lawrie's birthplace – that house at Moniaive?'

'Now look here' Frank said sternly 'forget strolling and house visits. This is going to be the 'Big Walk' remember, and I think we ought to give Loch Enoch our best go.'

Rex spoke at last 'Forget it. Just thinking about heights makes me dizzy. Highest peak? Highest loch? No way.'

'No sheer drops, no precipices or gorges – promise. It's not like that. This is a loch we're talking about. Just a walk up a gentle slope to a loch with silver strands for God's sake.' Frank was trying to be reassuring and defuse anxiety.

We'd had a bottle of Beaujolais, I was feeling mellow. I was almost convinced. Rex just shrugged.

'So that's settled then.' Frank drained his coffee cup. 'I'll go and plan our ascent. The highest loch – it'll be something to tell people... like.... 'the conquest of....' He couldn't quite bring himself to say 'Everest.'

'Think I'll have an early night' Rex said. It was 8 30. I suspected he was going to watch television in his room.

I'd noticed, vaguely, as we'd had our cheese, that the dining room had been filling up with a large party of middle aged women. Our waitress nodded at them and told us 'Women's Guild – annual dinner dance.' Dinner – yes... but dance? I turned back to the remains of my coffee and the merits of the 'Awful Hand' versus the bonnie braes of Maxwellton.

The pleasant gentle buzz of the ladies' chat swirled round me. I nibbled a bit more of my cheese biscuit. I was getting addicted to Lockerbie cheddar and thought of the silver strands but was rudely interrupted by a loud blast of an electric organ, which I hadn't noticed before. Women in couples swept suddenly in their floral magnificence on to a cleared circle surrounded by the tables and started to cha cha cha. The lady organist, in formal black, played exuberantly.

I drained my coffee quickly and attempted a getaway but sashaying towards me, in time to the music and blocking my way, came somebody's grandmother: she was looking at me and her body language said 'Come on, we're going to enjoy a bit of boogie together.'

I became interested in the tartan curtains behind me and studied them intently but it was no good. She couldn't see me sitting on my own. I looked sad, she said. God, she felt sorry for me and besides she was related to me.

'How so?' Fatal mistake, I was looking at her now and speaking to her.

'Your tie. Ma grandmother was a McGregor too – from Crieff.' Curse my unlucky selection taken at random. 'Come on – try a wee cha cha.' She held her arms open in what was meant to be an inviting gesture then played her trump card. 'It's ma birthday.'

'So sorry, can't dance – two right feet.'

'That's all *right* then.' She laughed at her own weak joke. 'I'll lead' and she pulled me to my feet while her friends laughed and cheered. I thanked God that Frank and Rex weren't there to witness this fiasco. Surreal moments while I stumbled round, looked at sardonically by the beady eyes of a moose head.

The Latin-American medley was coming to a close with a Samba. I'd been way out of my depth and wondered how I could beat a hasty retreat but my partner clung to me purposefully. The organist announced 'Highland Waltz – this is an 'excuse me'.'

That sounded promising. I was more than ready to say 'excuse me' and vanish but 'Oo, you'll be in great demand.' The tune was moody, sentimental and familiar – many were singing as they converged on me. I looked round for a way of escape and saw Frank, standing by the door, watching. Mortification complete.

But – what was this?

Stuffing his map in his pocket, he swiftly joined me and grasped my partner, whirling her away with 'Can anyone join in?'

After the 'Highland Waltz' and a 'Crashing White Sergeant,' we felt we'd done our bit and retired to some applause.

I owed Frank one. Loch Enoch it was.

* * *

SIXTEEN

The day of the Big Walk started out well. I didn't oversleep; Frank's boils were under control by now. He'd discovered a route up to Loch Enoch, provided we could borrow a forestry key to unlock an essential gate and we were confident that we'd thrown the Price-Kettle off our tracks.

Rex didn't appear for breakfast but our friend the bald archaeologist did. Errol's face above his embryonic beard was that certain shade between lime and lemon which I sometimes use to paint foliage on perspectives – a good colour for plants but not so good for skin.

'Rough night?' I asked.

'Puff ball mushrooms or it could have been the seaweed soup… or the winkle and grass stew.' The remembrance of these made him turn away and I thought he might vomit. I thought I might too.

'We played 'Adverbs' afterwards. I threw up and guess what, they all sat around saying things like 'nauseatingly,…. sickeningly…..disgustingly…" They thought it was part of the game and that I was acting my head off.'

He collected some orange juice.

'So… I couldn't make the scavenger hunt project this morning. The others went off at 6 am. Head hunted someone from the other team to take my place. He took a sip of juice and sighed 'I've not made the grade.'

'You'll be able to catch up later,' I said.

'Raft construction this afternoon.' He sighed. 'Followed by abseiling, building a shelter followed by campfire charades tomorrow. Tell me more about this little family museum,' trying to think of something more pleasant.

But I couldn't. I said 'Cheers and Good luck' but I hadn't quite seen the last of him.

Frank had gone to see about getting permission to use the forestry key and to order a picnic lunch, check on his miniature gas stove, sticking plasters and supply of mints, toffees and pastilles. I decided to try a phone call to Jane, then remembered it would be the middle of the night in Vancouver.

We'd told the hotel airily that we wouldn't be taking the rooms for another night as we didn't know where we'd be. This was true: we wanted to be free to roam where fancy took us.

Rex appeared: the elation of the previous day had vanished. He looked pale and furious – a vicious crow and I wondered if we could leave him behind. This holiday was a joint free zone: Frank and I didn't do that sort of stuff – not a whiff of a spliff. Richard Hannay –

yes. Sherlock Holmes.. no. But Rex? Disloyally, I realised it wouldn't take much more to make me side with Kate. He had a limited repertoire of swear words but went through it quickly on the start of our drive. He was on third repeats when I shook him by his scrawny shoulders (easy as I was sitting in the back), called him a miserable sod and used a few words from my own repertoire.

He seemed surprised. Frank brought the car to a stop on the empty road. 'I can't drive with this going on. What the hell is it with you, Rex?'

'I've got worries – huge worries.'

'Tough' I wasn't sympathetic.

'I know you're going through a bad time with Kate' Frank said. Rex gave a short sarcastic laugh.

'We've all got worries for God's sake' I put in 'Where's the next significant job coming from – staff problems – mortgage. I could go on… and Frank here… he has worries.' Couldn't think of any big ones off hand. He probably worries where his next meal is coming from but I wasn't going to say that.

'So get real. Stop being a pain.'

'Look, you guys would like me to jump train, right?'

Yeess! My fist almost punched the air but Frank wasn't having any of it.

'Forget it. It's Thursday today. We have to go back on Sunday. The weather's fine – we're having a great time. Sit on your problems, Rex, and let's get back on track – right?'

A grudging 'Right' came from Rex. Pity – but I suppose Frank was right.

We had just one dodgy moment before we picked up the key at the remote cottage and that was when Frank asked me when Jane was due back.

'Two weeks on Saturday. Slight complications as she wants to see her Godfather in Rio de Janeiro on the way back – it means taking a Pan-Am plane and then a...'

'Oh no...' A groan from Rex which I could only put down to thoughts on his own mental state so I pandered to him and changed the subject.

'So how's the 'sword cycle' going? Manage to get anything down last night?' I was going to add 'or were you watching television?' but stopped myself just in time.

'It's .... coming together' he said grudgingly but then opened up a bit 'I've a nice little solo in mind for Cromwell at the end of Act 2 – a nightmare song. The ruins rise up against him. It's a metaphor for destruction and revival.'

There might be one or two problems staging it. Special effects could be fun. We discussed how it could be done and this brought us to the bumpy track up to the cottage.

The padlocked gate was a slow mile or two further up the track. We unlocked it, passed through, then along what seemed miles of bumps up the forestry road until Frank decided he'd found the place to park at Back Hill of Bush and we started the walk.

We crossed a burn called Gala Lane and followed another which came down a steep ravine between Dungeon Hill and Mulwharchar. Frank had worked out from his map that this was the best route to Loch Enoch and we didn't argue. There seemed to be no cliffs or crags to cause a giddy turn in Rex if we stuck to this plan. Our feet felt more or less comfortable at this stage, our rucksacks not too heavy and Frank had promised us some real coffee when we reached the loch.

We'd only gone up about a hundred yards when we felt exhausted. The ruts caused by the forestry drainage system made the going hard and our feet ache. The sun beat down on us and we sank down feeling wrecked.

After a mint and a banana, Frank said 'This is ridiculous – come on – we've only been gone (he looked at his watch) half an hour.'

Slowly, unwillingly, we dragged ourselves up the ravine of scrubby grass trying to encourage each other with thoughts of Mountain Blend coffee made with pure loch water – forget about acid rain– magnificent views, the mysterious silver strands, a long rest….

The hills on either side rose up but gave no shelter from the sun. On one of our many stops we listened to the silence and knew we were completely alone – more alone than that day we'd walked along the old railway track. There was not a sign of civilisation here once we'd climbed beyond the forestry tracks. I think the isolation got to Rex – there'd be no signal on his mobile even if he'd thought of using it.

'Can't go any further' he said in a broken voice.

'We must be nearly there now. Just thirty-nine steps' (Frank tried a little joke) but it was deceptive. We thought each hillock would be the last, only to discover another one higher up.

'Coffee' he promised.

At 2 o'clock, a mist came down. The peaks of Dungeon Hill and Mulwharchar disappeared from time to time. We knew we must be near the loch and made a last effort, staggering with our feet feeling like lumps of lead.

'Remember Robert the Bruce and the spider.' Wrong sort of context, Frank, but we knew what he meant and continuing his battle theme he spurred us on, promising us victory.

'This must be it' he announced when we could see no further ascent in front of us. We could see no loch either for a moment or two (and could only just make out each other) because of the mist. Then magically, everything changed. A slight puff of wind blew away the cloud and there was Loch Enoch spread out in front of us with higher hills surrounding it, rocks, scrub and when the sun appeared it lit up a beach of dazzling silver sand – the silver strands.

'We've done it! My God, we've done it!' Frank, the trimphant leader now. Everest? Forget it. 'What an achievement. Well done, you guys' – General congratulating his troops. 'And wasn't it worth it? All together now...'

I croaked 'Yeah' but Rex lay by the loch panting and speechless.

It really was worth it. When we'd recovered, we made a base camp. Frank, using a Union Jack handkerchief, improvised a flag, set up his gas stove and I went to fetch water with the billy can. Rex had managed to generate enough energy to light a cigarette and inhaled deeply, his eyes fixed on a distant spot of the tranquil water.

'Matches, matches' Frank called 'Rex, you lazy sod, come on, I said 'matches.''

'Sorry, just used the last one – are we eating now? I'll just put this out.' He went to stub out his cigarette but we both sprang at him and I rescued it, passed it to Frank. Huffs and puffs later, the stove sprang to life.

Our lunch; sandwiches {of Lockerbie cheddar – what else – and pickle), pieces of apple tart and some fruit was spread out like a banquet and we fell on it like starving troops. Never had coffee tasted so pure. The caffeine revived me enough to do a quick, misty watercolour – quick because the place could disappear again at any moment like Brigadoon. I was putting the finishing touches to our flag blowing bravely in an imaginary breeze, when Rex cried out 'My God!'

'What the hell is it?' He'd sighted a pack of wolves about to devour us? Or had he stubbed his toe on a rock? You could never be sure with Rex.

But it was neither. It was a brainwave.

'Halleluiah, Halle-bloody-luiah and Eureka!' He described, with shrill animation, the vision that had smacked him in the eye,. 'Act 1, Scene 1, curtain goes up and there's a shimmering lake, touch of mist, bags of atmosphere. A silver sword clutched by a hand appearing out of the arm of a silver robe rises up from the water – Excalibur!. A burst of plain song – Gregorian chant – or was Arthur pre-Christian? Perhaps the power of evil manifesting itself? A flash of lightning?'

Again, my sympathies were with the stage manager but at least Rex had come out of his brood if only temporarily.

Frank had woken with a start at Rex's cry. The haze was obscuring the other side of the loch now.

'Look, we ought to bury a time capsule here before we go,' he said rather grandly, but apart from a sweet paper and a paper clip we couldn't come up with anything so we just buried those wrapped in a banana skin.

SEVENTEEN

The haze had turned into a pea souper which swirled
about us. We enjoyed the damp cool of it but it meant
that it took us a good hour before we struck what we
thought must be the right track for the descent. There
were no familiar landmarks to show us the way. At one
point, Rex thought he recognised a rock, which
resembled a face but then changed his mind 'The chin's
too long.' All we knew was that we were going down,
otherwise we were lost. Once we heard what sounded
like a light aircraft flying overhead 'That'll be P-K
hunting us down' Frank said but didn't add that P.K.
might have been given a surprise welcome as things stood.

Stumbling, staggering and with ruined kneecaps, we
eventually struck straight terrain and with the mist
swirling away as quickly as it had come, we saw more
forestry drainage rut systems in front of us and then like
a mirage, the road curling away over moor land. No sign
of the car.

Frank's cheap compass didn't work, no signals from mobiles so we tossed for it.

I chose 'right.' Rex said he was sure we should have chosen left. The sun came out again and Frank offered us the last of his mint cake and tried to rally our spirits, reminding us of people who'd been lost in the desert or in the Antarctic and found against all the odds in the nick of time. I'd rather he'd kept quiet. But St Jeeves – the patron saint of stupid bastards who go off into the wild totally unprepared – was with us that day and round a turn in the road, there she was – our home from home, our sanctuary, our saviour. Despite the blisters on our blisters, we attempted a half run, drunkenly weaving our way towards the bottle green dot and when we reached her we patted her dusty bonnet.... We praised her beauty, her general reliability and promised her toppings up of oil, petrol, distilled water for her battery, air in her tyres, anything she wanted but alas, it turned out her name was Perfidia. Fed up with waiting around, she threw a huge sulk and died on us. And that might have been that. Frank's spirits, along with his energy level had dropped by now and he was silent. There was a great and terrible silence, which we didn't care for now. Well, we could sleep in the car and wouldn't freeze – it wouldn't be much worse than our caravan experience but we had no food or drink. I found myself deeply envying the C.R.S./D.I.P.I. teams with their puffball mushrooms and seaweed soup.

Frank got out of the car and kicked the wheel and that was that. No forestry work would be going on here for some weeks we'd been told.

Nothing else for it but repair our feet and prepare for a long, long trek to God knew where for help the next day and settling back to listening to Frank reading the '39 Steps' until it grew dark.

I thought light-headedness due to lack of food (Rex had only had 2 cups of coffee at the picnic of distant memory) might have caused him to say suddenly. 'Did you know that Borodin was a gynaecologist?'

Er – no, neither of us did but it was a reasonably interesting fact.

'Know any other nuggets?' I asked. Anything to keep our minds off food.

'Yes. Wagner's favourite key was the key of E flat… and … wait for it… he was inspired to write Lohengrin when he heard the sound of rushing water in his hotel bedroom one night – probably someone in the next room running a bath…'

'Or flushing the loo.' Frank suggested.

Rex scowled. I racked my brain and came up with 'Rasputin was the original chat line freak – loved nothing more than a bit of hot gossip on the phone with his mates.'

'Never'

'True…. And' I thought of another gem, architectural this one 'Gilbert, of Gilbert and Sullivan, had a house called 'Grimsdyke.'

'So?'

' – and in it, he had a room called 'The Flirtorium'. Frank your turn.'

He said he found it difficult to think properly with his brain starved of food but after a while, he remembered something he'd heard once.

'I think I've got it right – at Arthur Conan-Doyle's school there was a boy called Holmes – Sherlock Holmes *and* two brothers called – guess what -?'

'Watson?' I volunteered.

'No – Moriaty.'

'Well, waddya know?'

'Tchaikovsky travelled in the U.S.A. – visited the Big Apple.' Rex said.

'I imagined him permanently stuck in Russia. Sounds far too modern' Frank sounded aggrieved. 'Anyway, trump this – 'Just William' was based on Richmal Crompton's brother, Jack.'

'I think that's fairly common knowledge' I said.

'Ah, but during the second World War, when he was in the Air Force, he served under Air Commodore Cecil Wigglesworth, who'd been one of the inspirations for Biggles – and so…. The real William Brown met the real Biggles!' and he paused for effect. This fact was quite good. We were on a roll now.

'I believe you could get take-aways in Charles II's reign' Rex said 'Pepys mentions it somewhere.'

This was cruel, though. The mention of 'take aways' conjured up curries, Chinese, fish and chips, anything. We wondered what seventeenth century fast food consisted of…. Suet puddings, meat dumplings – luscious syllabubs…

We had to change the subject and I dredged up from who knows where 'Nijinsky was a married man.' We all fell silent and contemplated this fact. Either the other two were so startled by this information or they were trying to work out who Nijinsky was that they didn't hear a slight sound coming from far away. I looked round and saw a matchbox model of an old Fordson tractor bumping along the road in the distance but coming towards us. I thanked St Jeeves again and shook the others by the shoulders, then we spread out across the track, waving and shouting as it drew nearer.

'Nae problem' Jack McNichol said when we explained. He was an optimist and I blessed him for a true Samaritan as he not only towed us in stately fashion back to his farm, miles up a lonely glen, but offered us lodging for the night. He was living on his own now he explained and liked a wee bit o company now and again. Half his flock of sheep were beyond the track we'd taken up to the loch and he'd been on his way with Muster, his elderly sheepdog to check up on them and again 'nae problem' that he'd have to do his checking up next day now.

'Ye're in luck' he said. He'd done his weekly shop in Newton Stewart the day before and his larder was well stocked and we had a second breakfast.

Jack's television set had broken down 6 weeks ago and he hadn't got round to having it repaired yet. 'I dinna miss it – apart from Children's News Round.' He did have a telephone though, and a married daughter in Canada. 'The wee lassies (his grand daughters) already go tae Reels classes. We speak once a week. I'm on cheap rate.' They lived in Victoria, near Vancouver, and I worked out that it would be about midday there while we ate our meal. I hardly liked to ask after all he'd done already but...

'Nae problem. You phone your lassie this verra minute.' And I got straight through to Jane's sister, Anna.

'Not easy to talk just now' she said 'I'm looking after Livvie and she needs to go to the loo – I've bought her this cute little seat that fits over it and – yes, I'm coming' I could hear my daughter thousands of miles away chunnering away with her scribble talk while here was I in a lowland glen. It was too far.

'Where's Jane?'

'You've missed her. She's out with Chris and I don't know when she'll be back.'

'Give her my love.'

'Look, she needs to talk to you. All right, I'm coming. Have to go. Bye.'

This was unsatisfactory. Who the hell was Chris and what did she need to talk to me about? I popped the old fashioned cosy, shaped like a crinoline lady back over the telephone and shoved a couple of coins under her skirt.

Jack's small farm house was dark and low ceilinged, book lined inside and full of furniture – so we all had a place to sit, enjoying cocoa laced liberally with whisky, while he enjoyed the novelty of an audience for his tales reaching back over the centuries, tales he'd heard from his grandfather and father, who'd each sat in their turn in the rocking chair, which he now occupied. Raiders, levellers, smugglers, all cropped up and we heard about 'Old Mortality' who made it his life's work to tend and restore tombstones of the Covenanters persecuted in the 17th century for the cause of religious liberty – travelling the Galloway countryside on his white pony.

More blood shed in the name of religion.

Listening to Jack and concentrating hard, helped to take my mind off Jane. Everything was all right I told myself. Everything was all right.

Rex's eyes were half closed – a sign that a) he might be falling asleep or b) he was thinking of plagiarising some of the dramatic content of these savage tales for his libretto.

'You know, quite seriously, you should get all this down on tape,' Frank said, when Jack drew breath for a moment, 'or perhaps a book – a pamphlet or something,' he amended.

'Och – thrillers are my line' Jack said 'Ma publisher's breathing down ma neck just now.'

'Publisher?;' Frank echoed faintly.

Jack pointed to a pile of books on a nearby table. Judging by the lurid cover on the top one, they were racy, pacey, contemporary airport shop fodder.

'Jack Carson – that's me. There's some talk of putting one on the telly but it's probably all blather. Must be getting back to work noo.' He heaved himself out of the rocker. 'Hope the sound o' ma typewriter won't keep you laddies awake.'

* * *

EIGHTEEN

The man from a garage in Newton Stewart arrived about 10 am and diagnosed carburettor trouble – dirt in petrol. He fixed up Perfidia in about ten minutes but advised a look at the fan belt and a check up back at his base before we did much more mileage. It was all going to cost a bit ('Ma let her R.A.C. membership lapse' Frank said) but we were just thankful to be mobile again.

Jack said he'd return the forestry key – he had one himself. How on earth to repay him for all his kindness to us, complete strangers? It went beyond money.

'Och – it was nothing' he said. 'I've enjoyed your company. I like the solitary life, mind, but noo an' agen it's good to see folks and mebbe' and here he raised his eyebrows over laughing eyes 'mebbe ye've gi'en me a scheme for ma next yarn.' He gave us one of his yarns with the title 'Dead by Nine' and came out to the car with us.

I was still using Frank's plus fours as a rough cushion

and I took them out and gave them a good shake watching while dust, dirt, sprigs of heather were scattered like a plague of locusts.

'Man, that's a fine bit o' tweed' Jack said admiringly. 'I used to have some troosers like that years ago. I miss them still.'

He was a braw, big-bellied man. Well what could Frank do?

'Take them' he said.

* * *

I turned and waved to Jack until he and Muster were out of sight and we followed the rescue car to Newton Stewart. We left the car there for an hour during which time Frank filled his pockets with particulars of local properties, which would join those he'd gathered in Castle Douglas and Kirkcudbright.

There were craft shops and woollen mill shops in the town and I tossed up between a funky tam o' shanter and a gem stone brooch for Jane and a miniature tartan kilt of many colours and a large stuffed Scottie dog wearing a tartan coat for Livvie. Then there was a subtle watercolour of a local scene, a whisky liquor, honey. I bought them all. Oh and a long, soft woollen scarf – pale turquoise, Jane's favourite colour. I pushed those ominous words 'needs to talk to you' to the back of my mind again. This was something I'd deal with later. I've never liked the phone as a means of communication – too direct and no eye contact. I wondered if, when everyone had face to face mobiles, it would make a difference.

I arranged my spoils on the table at the café where we met for lunch, but there was a lack of interest in it all except for the whisky liquor. Rex had bought two newspapers, one 'the Financial Times', and busied himself flicking over the pages.

We'd thought Frank had had enough of the simple life after yesterday but over steak and kidney pie he dropped a bombshell.

'Look, I didn't drag my tent all the way up here for nothing.'

Oh no, I could guess what was coming. I caught Rex's eye and we groaned simultaneously.

'I think we did pretty well yesterday.' He was encouraging his troops again. 'We rose to the challenge...'

'....and were not found lacking' I finished for him. God, he sounded like an old W.W.1 movie.

'Well, a night's camping will be a piece of cake... Talking of which...'

* * *

Eventually, we struck a bargain with him. O.k. a night under canvas – nowhere too remote – not too far from a road – followed by our last night, on Saturday, to be spent in a half way decent hotel with at least one rosette.

After having his wicked way with the tent, Frank was happy for us to think of a suitable site to pitch it.

The ground was dry, the good weather held and we didn't think we'd have a problem but we couldn't agree. Rex had the idea of camping in the grounds of the

'Barreough Hotel' (good food? Access to television? Possible company of Courtney?) but Frank chimed in saying that wouldn't be in the spirit of the thing.

I suggested a farm – fresh eggs, supply of water, milk and so on but Frank was stern 'No relying on others. We'll take all our provisions with us, find a stream, light a fire.. be completely self-sufficient.' After coffee we still hadn't come to any decision and Frank had switched his interest to the sheaf of papers which he'd spread all over the table and was now totally absorbed in sorting and sifting. These were his precious collection of particulars of local properties he'd culled during our stay. He pored over them, now and again shouting 'Bloody Hell' or 'I just don't believe it.' Rex and I broke off our campsite debate, which was going nowhere, and started shuffling the papers ourselves. Of course it was the prices compared to London ones which were causing the expletives.

Frank stabbed at one 'Just look at this!' He read out '17th century ruined Mansion House in 60 acres and stretch of the Garvie River... blah, blah, blah. Offers over... you won't believe this. Guess!'

We guessed.

'Nowhere near.'

'Too high or too low?'

'High'

We tried again.

'No'

'Give up – come on.'

'Halve your last guess' Frank said triumphantly and stabbed again at the particulars.

'60 acres!' I said.

'17th Century' Rex said

'A river!'

'It must be a mistake.'

'But it's a ruin – probably cost treble that just to do up a fraction.' Me, trying to be practical.

'Look' Frank said and we guessed what was coming 'We've got to go and see this place.'

'Yeah!.'

The property, 'Upper Knocksting' was being sold by one of the Newton Stewart agents. 'Chase, McCraig, McCathie.' There had been some interest at first. 'Someone was thinking of running it as a theme park and games centre with canoeing etc.' we were told by Liz Chase. The house had originally been owned by Lord Lauriston who had moved to Ireland and it hadn't been lived in since the 1940s. Some relative had had a shot at restoring it 30 years ago and had taken down a wing… and lead from the roof had been stolen. 'Present owner's a bit of an eccentric – joined a commune.'

The woman seemed uninterested in why we should want a viewing although Frank muttered something about 'fishing interests' and she said 'I'm afraid there's no one free to show you round this afternoon. Would you mind that?'

'Nae problem' we all rushed to say and we were given some keys and directions of how to get there.

Frank held up the keys 'We'll get them back to you by five o'clock. How's that?'

'Upper Knocksting' was up in the hills, beyond New Galloway and there was a good road, the A712, following the Palnure Burn, Clatteringshaws Loch by Bruce's Stone, fir plantations and open moorland – but before we set off we needed to buy provisions for our night in the wild, wherever that might be.

'Scottish cuisine?' Rex suggested.

'O.K., O.K., tempt me' Frank said.

'Well, haggis of course and that thing they do with turnips and potatoes – knock it up with butter, don't they? Salmon to start... and I had a great pud once – toasted oatmeal, cream, whisky, Gaelic coffee, of course....'

Ambitious stuff, this. I thought of our one ring gas stove and small elderly pan.

We hoped the cream we bought wouldn't go off in the heat. The butter was already runny by the time we'd staggered back to the car with our load of supplies having added more whisky, potato cakes, shortbread and something called 'tablet.' We remembered extra matches this time... oh, and kippers for breakfast.... And some herbs Rex insisted on buying.

The tweed trousers had gone but there was less room than ever in the car and we stretched our legs with relief when we arrived at the ruined gate lodge that the agent had described standing on a road to nowhere. Key number one unlocked a padlock attached to a chain linking a pair of high rusty wrought iron gates. On either side of the gates were pillars upon which crouched a pair of sad looking lions, both minus front paws, who gazed down on us. 'Could use a good bit of oil' Frank said as we pushed and shoved. Rex obliged with some of his extra virgin olive oil. Clogged up with weeds and ivy, the gates obviously hadn't been opened for months despite the agent's optimistic visions of paint balling and entrepreneurial derring do.

Putting our combined weight into the effort and with creaks and groans (ours) they eventually and reluctantly opened and we drove through – not closing them behind us in case we couldn't open them again.

It became hard to see which was the old drive and which was just undergrowth. We could only tell we were on the right track by the potholes and Frank grew seriously worried about his 'Ma's springs.'

We came to a small loch on the right, hardly any water visible through a forest of bullrushes.

'Must be the curling pond and over on the left's the burn.' Frank had stopped the car, which sighed with relief, and referred to the particulars 'Probably dried up with the heat.'

'Haven't we all?' Rex foraged for some cans of luke warm fizz.

We left the car under the shade of a huge copper beech and made our way towards a five bar gate, locked, but we pushed it open after undoing the padlock and one of the bars fell off.

The overgrown drive now curved round between a hilly paddock and part of an avenue of magnificent ancient oaks and after about a quarter of a mile we reached the house, set against a distant backdrop of pale blue hills and stood stock still.

* * *

NINETEEN

The sun, which had been blazing away merrily all day, suddenly went behind a cloud as if to accentuate the desolate appearance of the ruined grey-stone façade. The twisted, barley-sugar chimneys looked poised to collapse at any moment and any windows still unbroken were almost obliterated by brambles and saplings: some were shuttered. Blind and forlorn it looked and I couldn't wait to open that bow shaped front door and rummage around in this huge, quirky house with its Victorian Dutch gables but date stone marked 1598. Looking at it, I couldn't imagine how the rooms had been planned but Frank and Rex were striding out over the grounds, impatient to see other intriguing attractions mentioned in the particulars – a small bridge, reputed to have been walked over by Mary, Queen of Scots and a cave in the glen by the side of the river, which had been used by Covenanters hiding from their persecutors.

'The house can wait,' Frank called back over his shoulder. Well, o.k. and he had the keys so I hurried after them and together we explored this Shangrila – a forgotten world.

The river could still be heard despite the drought and we were drawn towards it, down past crumbling terraces, along greened over narrow tracks smelling of garlic with woods of delicate silver birch rising up a hill on the right. Through a jungle of giant rhododendrons and then way down below, we saw the Garvie, tumbling and frothing over rocks. We scrambled down through dappled sunlight to get nearer and sat on the trunk of a fallen tree by the waterfall letting the sound wash over us..... Utter peace – and to think, all this could be ours for less than the price of a crash pad in London. It didn't bear thinking about. None of us spoke for a while.

'Liz Chase said a salmon was once caught here,' Frank said at last and sighed.

I spied a cleft in the bank opposite.

'Covenanter's cave?'

It was an effort to move – we'd been mesmerised by the river.

'Could be' Frank said, heaving himself up.

By leaping, or treading gingerly, from one large stone to another, where the water was more shallow we managed to reach the other side and stepped on to shingle, beneath the gaping dark hole. The cavern seemed larger now, though narrow, and we hauled ourselves up, grabbing tree roots and rocks. At the entrance we looked in. Rex lit a match but this was as far as he could manage – 'Bats... claustrophobic... no way' he puffed.

We could smell the fear and something worse – putrefying flesh.

'Wild cats – they have them round here' Frank said.

'Wolves' I said. I'd remembered reading recently that they'd been sighted in Scotland.

'Well o.k. we can tick off the cave' Frank said swiftly 'Now for Queen Mary's Bridge.'

We found it up nearer the house – ancient, mossy stoned and leading over the sluggish burn to some ruined stables.

'God – the scope of this place, never mind paint balling or theme park' Frank marvelled.

Rabbits dodged out of our way – shocked by this rude intrusion into their personal arcadia– as we battled our way back through more rhododendrons and emerged at the side of the house. I could see where a wing had been demolished and was mad with impatience to see the inside.

Frank turned the key in the padlock. The shuttered door creaked open and we breathed in the dank, stale air.

'Pooooh phew! Christ whatever's died in here?' Frank asked.

'Well, I expect your place wouldn't come up smelling of roses if it hadn't been lived in since the nineteen forties' I said and tried to wrench open one of the shutters to get more light, but the hinges broke off and the whole thing crashed to the floor.

'That'll cost you something' said Rex cheerfully but at least we could see something of the room now. I'm used to looking at 'befores' (as in 'before restoration,' 'before conversion') in my job but I'd never seen anything like this 'before.' We were in a huge, lofty hall with very few touches of its former glory remaining. Piles of rubbish, broken boards and unrecognisable pieces of trashed furniture were strewn about or stacked high against peeling mouldering walls. A chipped china lavatory leant at a crazy angle on a broken table, unlikely forms of fungus hung in drapes. Graffiti were daubed on a wall – 'Bruce Rules O.K'– indoor re-enactment of Bannockburn, perhaps?

'Look, I'm going out for a smoke. Marvellous place for 'Murder in the Dark' but just not my scene' Rex said.

'But the atmosphere is perfect. Think Black Hole of Calcutta. You owe it to your libretto,' I said, but he wasn't persuaded and escaped.

Desolation and decay were everywhere.

We heard a fluttering noise and a creak.

'Come in, Miss Haversham!' Frank boomed: his voice echoed, then silence.

I scraped with my foot along the floor through layers of grime and saw what I knew would be there – blue and brown patterned tiles – and in the semi darkness I'd spotted some very old plasterwork in the ceiling.

'Come on' I said – I couldn't wait to see the rest of it.

'You carry on – I just need to graze… a bit of shortbread or something and I'll check on the cream' Frank said. So I completed the tour on my own. A tour leading to a maze of rooms – large, small, old kitchens with broken tiles, wires hanging forlornly, pipes leading nowhere, doors wrenched off…. All ruined, torn to pieces and covered with more than half a century's droppings of birds and beasts mingled together like complicated stuccowork.

Some of the windows were shattered, providing easy access and making nonsense of the padlock.

I was ferreting around behind an attic staircase and still trying to make sense of the layout when I heard Frank way down below.

'Hey! Come *on* – got to get those keys back remember!' and I reluctantly joined him.

'Look – just run around a bit in the fresh air, will you?'

'Sure.' I probably needed to freshen up.

'We might just have time to call at The Grannoch for a quick one on the way. We promised Dunc we'd look in, remember?'

I could have had another half hour getting the feel of the old place and the memory of the literary innkeeper had nearly faded from my mind now, but I was dehydrated, dry and dusty and ready for a cool beer.

We rattled back down the drive. While I'd been giving the house the once over, Frank had had another look round the land and was bursting with ideas. 'Bit of shooting – you could form a syndicate, fishing in the river, fish farm in the curling pond.... Do up the lodge and rent it out, B & B in the main house and that's just for starters....'

'Yeah, you could have guides dressed in plaid, giving tours of Mary Queen of Scots bridge... "follow in her very footsteps" and the auld Covenanter's cave – to the sound of bagpipes – and a stall selling wee Jeanie's homemade shortbread and whisky cake.' Rex had gone over the top but Frank wasn't really listening.

In my imagination, I was restoring the old house –

going through it room by room. It would have to be a virtual clean sweep indoors and starting again – it could be done but at a price that didn't bear thinking about. I knew Frank wasn't being serious but felt he needed a bit of professional advice.

'Don't even begin to think of it' I told him. 'It would cost a bomb, believe me' and I gave a rough outline of basic essentials; but he seemed far away, only saying that you could start with just one wing. I gave up and we all fell silent until just before we reached The Grannoch when Frank said 'We could all chip in – share it as a holiday home – brilliant!'

Rex just said 'Get real' and 'As if.'

'Nice try, but I've enough trouble keeping my head above water as it is without saddling myself with a ravenous monster like that' I said.

'I thought you of all people would appreciate a challenge like that – restoration of a grand old house. Saving it for the Nation and so on,' he said sulkily.

'Well a) I don't think it's quite in that league and b) I haven't won the lottery recently.'

He lightened up a bit 'I think it would make a fantastic place for us to camp tonight. I'll phone Liz Chase from Dunc's and say we'll drop the keys in tomorrow.

He was keen to have another look, obviously.

I said I wasn't sure about insurance and boring things about trespass laws but he swept all this aside. We arrived at the pub and he went straight to the phone.

* * *

TWENTY

I don't think I'm doing Duncan an injustice when I say no flicker of recognition passed over his face when we went in – but then, he'd had a very busy week. He immediately put on a good act though and welcomed us. 'What'll it be?'

Frank went off to do his phoning and Rex and I ordered some beers asking Duncan to join us. He told us that 'the people from the telly' were in the area and that he himself might be called upon to give an account of literary associations in the area.

'Only two minutes, mind, but a wee bit of fame, ye ken.'

'Och, that's grand' I responded and looked round for Rex to endorse my enthusiasm but he'd gone over to a corner seat with his drink, having seen a familiar face.

'Flora!' I heard him say, with his useful memory for names 'this is a surprise.'

Duncan had turned away to serve others so I found

a seat near to Rex but not near enough to cramp his style and listened in.

'How's the fishing?' he continued with his wooing technique, but he'd backed a loser here.

'Don't even mention it' she said, scowling 'You don't fish do you?'

Now I could see that Rex was torn here, between a boast about the Whinyeon trout he'd caught and caution due to her bitter tone. He compromised with a slight movement of the head and a gulp of beer.

'I mean,' she went on 'one tries to be grown up about these things – share hobbies and all that stuff but do I look the sort of person who'd sit for three hours at a time just looking at a small patch of water?'

'Not at all' Rex said soothingly 'How about another?' nodding at her empty glass.

'No thanks, I've had three already. Just how snoring boring can you get? My hair's a fright – it's breezy out in the middle of some of these lochs. My skin's shrivelled; I've run out of my moisturiser. Thank God I found out what he was like in time. We were going to get engaged, you know.' She gave a nasty laugh 'No – Tim and I we're all washed up now.'

'Does Tim know about this?'

'Not as such.'

'Where is he?' Rex asked cautiously.

'Oh, he's off trying for a salmon on some river or other.'

Rex relaxed. 'What an oik.'

'Of course, I would have gone straight back to London but there's a party tomorrow night – one of

Tim's uncles is having a big bash, might be a giggle and I could certainly do with one.'

'This party…..' Rex said but she hadn't finished mouthing off about Tim.

'Do you know, we were out on some remote Godforsaken loch yesterday – not a sound – nothing – no conversation or anything like that – and a group of people suddenly arrived on the bank and began trying to make a couple of rafts for Christ's sake. Anyway there was fun – bit of animation. Any normal person would have been pleased by the diversion. I certainly was, but Tim? He was furious and rowed us to the other side, but amazingly, would you believe it, one of these weird looking rafts was launched – people actually got on it and I cheered along with them. Well, they paddled and splashed and came right over to us, laughing their heads off. A really good giggle. I threw them a couple of cans. A good looking bald fella nearly fell in trying to catch them. Of course, Tim spoilt it all. Don't think I've ever seen anyone so furious. Just goes to show, you never really know people deep down, do you?'

Rex made sympathetic noises and moved closer.

'About this party…'

She looked at her watch 'Must wash my hair. Thanks for lending an ear' and she gazed into Rex's eyes. 'I'll see you around.'

'Tomorrow night?'…. he persisted.

'Oh… you know… reels, huge house, huge drinks bill- you know the sort of thing.' She gave a smile and a little wave of her fingers and nearly bumped into Frank as she left the bar.

'That's settled then – keys back tomorrow. Hi, Dunc care to join us?' Frank got himself a drink, looking pleased with himself 'What do you know about Upper Knocksting?' he asked Duncan.

'Upper Knocksting? Fine property, my father used to say. Old Lord Lauriston wouldna recognise it now – derelict, they say.'

'You can say that again. It's for sale – we went there this afternoon.'

'Aye, it's bin for sale a good monny years. The great nephew, Guy Lauriston-Laurie lives in a shepherd's cottage over at that commune by Minnigaff. He came into the property recently but doesn't want anything to do wi' it. 'Share n' share alike's' his motto – everyone equal and all that. Has a black girl friend, verra attractive, and a string o' bairns. Still keeps in touch wi' one or two of his friends frae the auld days if there's a chance o' a dram or two. It's haunted, of course, Bothwell......' but the bar was filling up, people getting impatient, and he turned aside.

'We were thinking of camping'.... Frank started to say but he was hardly listening.

'Mind ye call by again, soon' he shouted.

'Cheers.' Frank raised his glass then tapped the barometer as we left.

'Don't like the look of that' I said, but someone coming through the door said cheerily 'Been broken for years.'

* * *

On the way back we checked over our list of essentials for our night under canvas. If we'd forgotten something vital, it would have been just too bad – there was no shop within miles.

We went through the rigmarole of the keys and gates. Shafts of late afternoon sun picked up the eyes of the second pair of lions, who glared unpleasantly.

While I had serious misgivings about our chances of having an enjoyable night – good food, good sleep etc.– there was comfort in the thought of the Gordon Arms where we'd booked rooms for our last night.

The kippers were starting to smell. We put them, the cream, butter and haggis down by the stream with a small piece of slate over the top and put some cans in a pool of shallow water to cool.

Frank suggested we dig a hole for the loo but it was too hot and we had no spade.

After these boy scout considerations, we found a reasonably flat piece of ground which wasn't covered in thistles or brambles, and hauled the tent off the roof rack of the car, which we'd left a little nearer the house this time.

It was a very old tent, the fabric cracked and brittle with age and from exposure for days to fierce sun. It also had a couple of patches and a slight rip – not a very promising shelter for the night but perhaps a bit better than the ones the Crass Dippies' would create. Or perhaps not, as their raft building had obviously been so successful.

Frank was proud of the end result – the tent sagged in the middle and there were not enough pegs. I remembered a hint I'd read somewhere about using bananas but just got a 'Try being helpful,' from Frank.

We put in the groundsheet and sleeping bags, which had been stuffed in the car boot, and thought about some supper. We looked at Rex... Salmon, haggis, pudding we'd been promised among other things. All this from a gas ring and one pan.

'It may take a while' he hedged, 'Actually I've never dealt with a haggis before.' He fetched it from the burn as if it were some live creature and gingerly placed it on a plastic plate. We all looked at it. It was the first time I'd seen one at close quarters before and said it resembled a largish grey cannonball.

'Well, get on with it.' Frank's energy levels were causing concern again.

'It needs careful handling. They're liable to explode, you know.' Rex looked at it with respect.

'So, hey, what are you going to do with it – roast it, stew it, fry it... eat it raw or are we just going to sit around gazing at it?'

'No, no. Could be really dangerous to eat it raw – when you think what's in it,' Rex said hastily and mentioned one or two of the ingredients.

I said that I didn't wish to know any more and did he want any help with the veg.

So I peeled potatoes and cut up the turnip and collected water in the pan from the sluggish burn. I startled a small deer who was having a drink and watched it trot away on delicate legs. Another first.

The gas ring was lit – at least we'd have 'neeps.' Rex was still looking worried about the haggis and our confidence in him as chef was being eroded.

'I think it might work better with a proper camp fire.

Billycans strung up over it like cauldrons. I could cut the haggis in half and boil it.'

We gathered wood, bits of kindling, Rex sacrificed one of his newspapers, and because everything was so dry we soon had a good blaze. It was altogether too good a blaze; and I could see it getting out of hand and I suggested we put it out, which we did with difficulty by beating it with branches and dowsing it with small amounts of water carried in the billycans.

A distant but distinct rumble was heard.

'God, you *are* hungry' I said to Frank.

We'd been too busy to notice that it was no longer sunny and black clouds were gathering. Then there was a spot of rain followed by some more.

'In the tent!' Rex shouted.

'What about supper? Cut the bloody haggis in two and put it in with the turnips' Frank said angrily.

Rex popped his head out of the tent. 'I've been thinking about that and I don't think I can do it. Hey – this is the integrity of the haggis we're talking about here.'

This high-minded approach didn't go down well with Frank.

Rain was falling into the open pan of veg, which was nearly cooked by now.

'Well, what about the salmon then?' he yelled furiously.

'There's a bit of smoked salmon, if I can find it. By the way, there's a leak in the tent.

* * *

TWENTY ONE

The vivid flash of lightning lit up Rex's face showing all the terror of a hypnotised mongoose, and was followed by such a crash of thunder that I thought the huge chimneys must have toppled.

More rain.

We'd forgotten about rain – forgotten what it was like. Rain in the city is different anyway – you can always pop in somewhere to keep dry. You don't have weather in London. Here there was little shelter from the torrent. The tent was soon waterlogged. When the rain stopped for a moment there was a silence that was sinister, followed by another streak of lightning and then immediately, a clap of thunder overhead so loud the whole world seemed to shake.

'Better get out of here' Frank shouted.

'I've a thing about thunderstorms – just can't cope. Don't think I can move' Rex was crouched down at the back of the tent.

'Never mind all that. We'll be struck if we stay here or one of those huge beech trees will fall on us.'

He was rallying troops again but didn't forget vital provisions even under pressure. While we scrambled out of the tent he rescued a plastic bag and the pan of veg. Frank marches on his stomach.

We ran and just reached the house before the next flash. The key wouldn't turn properly.

'Break a window!' Frank commanded but there was no need, we had several broken windows to choose from. I fiddled with the catch of one and it swung open, we climbed through.

'This could be the worse of two evils – it's disgusting' Rex said.

He could be right, I thought, thinking of all those towering chimneys, but just told him to shut up.

I remembered the plan of the rooms and led the way, stumbling and cursing as we went, into the hall, where I'd spotted a fireplace earlier. The room was lit up briefly in all its degradation.

'A fire's what we need. Soon dry us out and we can get on with cooking.' Frank looked at Rex accusingly and put down the salvaged potatoes and turnips, boiled dry, on an upturned tea chest.

'It'll smoke' I warned 'years of birds' nests… birds…..' but this was dismissed and when we'd lit a fire of scraps of wood and rubbish it did smoke, badly, but some of it escaped upwards through two large holes in the ceiling. It gave us a little light and Frank rooted round in the plastic bag and produced plastic mugs and plates, a small pack of smoked salmon, a bottle of whisky, the 'tablet,' which sounded like an Old Testament stone, and the haggis.

'All's not lost. Look, mash the veg., put it on a plate. Cook the haggis in the pan and hey presto!'

'No water' said Rex. He looked away while Frank attacked the haggis with his penknife and hacked it into pieces.

'A fry up then. Mix everything together and fry it in butter.'

'Ah, no butter – it's by the burn with the cream and the kippers and there's no way I'm going out to fetch it!' Rex said firmly.

'We'll do without, then!' Desperate now, Frank threw the desecrated pieces of haggis into the pan, shook in a liberal amount of whisky, added the smoked salmon and put the pan over some embers. Haggis abuse for sure.

Coughing, our eyes stinging from the smoke, we hovered over our cauldron. The fire cast up grotesque shadows and we became the three witches from 'Macbeth.'

It's hard to describe the taste of our supper that night although Rex said he discovered some interesting bass notes: the chief flavour had to be smoke... but it was filling. 'Tablet' turned out to be toffee – delicious, but it brought Rex out in a frenzy of toothache and he had to dull the pain with more whisky.

'What happened to the shortbread?' Frank was unfailingly focused where food was concerned, 'and what about that pudding – what was it? Toasted oatmeal, cream, whisky?' But Rex just moaned.

The storm wasn't about to go away but the rain had eased off and Frank suggested a visit to our campsite to retrieve what we could of our supplies and our sleeping bags.

It was Robinson Crusoe salvaging what he could from his wrecked ship but we weren't so lucky – the kippers, cream and butter had gone: there were just a few scraps of paper to show they'd ever been there. I remembered the deer and the rabbits.

The thought of black coffee and shortbread didn't go very far towards geeing Frank up and the sleeping bags were sodden but we trudged back with them through another cloudburst with the gas ring, the coffee, some water and a bag of oatmeal and climbed through the window. We cursed Rex for letting the fire go down. He was still sitting, hunched up on a pile of rubble like a brooding gargoyle. He'd been brought low. It would take him a while to get over this holiday. It may take all of us a while, I thought. I'd cut my hand on a piece of broken glass and Frank still occasioned his limp from Dirk Hatterick's cave. We put another broken floorboard on the fire.

The coffee revived us a bit – we made it into Gaelic coffee with whisky – and thought of the hotel near Castle Douglas where we'd be spending the next night.

'Our last day tomorrow' I said. 'Must make it a restful one – wind down. I'll be happy to do some sketching... browsing... that sort of thing and an early night.' I looked at the others, hoping they wouldn't say what I thought they might say – but they did.

'Reels at Stewartston' Frank said firmly. 'Definitely on the agenda and non-negotiable.'

'Yeah – that redhead, Issy something or other's going – I sort of said I'd see her there.'

'Keys back to Liz Chase.'

'Dentist.'

'Clocking into hotel'

Oh, Hell.

'Look, we can't gatecrash a party. You can't reel with that leg and we can't reel, full stop as I said before and look at us!.' I was really trying.

'We'll attach ourselves to Tattie and, if you haven't forgotten, you and I managed a funky Dashing White Sergeant at the Barreough.'

'It may be black tie.' This was my trump card but Frank wasn't having any.

'Things are more relaxed nowadays.' He regarded us critically through the smoke. We looked a wild bunch. Sunburnt – even Rex now– hair longer and knotted, which even dressing for dinner at the Barreough hadn't tamed, our clothes and spares, unmentionable.

'Oh, come on, a scrub up and a touch of hair gel and you won't recognise us.'

'You know – this hall, done up, would be terrific for reels.'

I could see Frank, in his imagination, was hosting a party here and he fell silent.

Thunder was still rumbling around threateningly. I fell silent too. Of course, I could do more skulking, avoid the reels party, and have my early night. Then an imp whispered in my ear 'She's out with Chris' and I thought 'what the hell, why should I skulk?' I'd have myself a good time. I could 'go out' too.

Sparks flew out of the fire and I moved the steaming sleeping bags further back.

'Thirty-Nine Steps,' anyone?' Frank offered. It was a kind offer but the inadequate flickering light and eyes watering from the smoke made it difficult, and he reluctantly abandoned the idea.

It was getting late, it was peaceful and we felt drowsy, though not able to get comfortable.

'I've just thought of something!' Rex startled us out of our musings.

'What?' Wondering what revelation was coming and if it would be good or bad.

'That game we played before Jack picked us up. I've just thought of another one... Edward Grieg's real name was Edward Gregg – his father was Scottish.'

'Nice one' I said wearily but Frank was more interested.

'Changed his name. Well I suppose it suited him to sound Norwegian, living in Norway. Grieg ... Didn't he write that Scottish number – 'Fingal's Caves?'' Frank asked.

'No, Peer Gynt.'

'Peer Gynt wrote 'Fingal's Caves'. Right. It's coming back to me ... it goes something like ...' and he gave a loud blast of something unrecognisable, ending in a choking cough due to the smoke.

'Shut up!' I want to get some sleep.' Rex tried to rearrange his rubble.

Someone else hated Frank's singing as much as we did as, suddenly, a loud warning 'Ssshhh' startled us. It sounded reproving, like a furious nanny. It came again, 'Ssshh!'

No-one was there.

The singing stopped.

'Haunted!' mouthed Rex.

But Frank, with Boy Scout and twitchers background, said reassuringly.

'Barn owl, ticking us off … must be up there somewhere.' He waved an arm vaguely.

OK, we were ready to be reassured and too tired to challenge his theory.

TWENTY TWO

Later, with rain still lashing against the few remaining windowpanes and with drips coming down from the ceiling, Frank said glumly 'We left the car windows open, didn't we?'

'Try not to think about it' I said soothingly.

'I ought to go and close them, I suppose.' But we discouraged him. It was pitch dark now and a gale force wind rattled the shutters and whined down the chimney. I expected to hear one topple at any moment.

'It's all a bit like one of those novels, isn't it? Forces of darkness, wanderers through the Universe – mantles, cloaks of intrigue, lost souls, children searching for something on long, tedious journeys, evil strangers, destiny… you know the sort of thing…. Listen while I tell you…. He was straying into 'Noggin the Nog here.'

'…. And characters with silly names like Axel and Pyles' I took up the story in a light hearted way but the place was getting to us.

There was no chance of sleep – no soft surfaces to lean up against although Rex had hunkered down with one steaming sleeping bag against a tea chest.

'I suppose we could have a séance' Frank suggested. Not a good suggestion. There was enough Hammer House of Horror about the place as it was.

As we tried, unsuccessfully, to cosy up with stacks of tiles and old tin cans, there suddenly came an almighty crash that wasn't thunder.

To my shame, my first thought was – 'Bothwell.' I think we all thought 'Bothwell' but none of us said anything for a second, then Frank managed –

'Christ, you were right, a bloody chimney's collapsed.'

The wind died down briefly and then while we were still frozen in fright and indecision we heard slow, measured footsteps echoing on bare boards coming closer. Straining our eyes in the smoky darkness we saw the handle on a door near the fireplace turn very slowly, and watched like petrified stoats as the door creaked open. It stuck and was given a kick, something swore and it sounded human, … not a bird this time, which turned our yellow streak into a more blood red colour altogether.

Frank, using his sergeant major voice, called out.

'Who the hell's there?'

A whingey voice, which we recognised instantly answered.

'Don't you guys ever answer your front door bell?' and Mr Nasty shoved his way through piles of trash into the room. By the light of his torch we could see the glow of his pale hair. He was wearing one of those macs you buy from travel shops, dark with belt, and looked organised and in control.

So, P.K. had tracked us down and now he shone his torch at us one by one…. Prisoners, humiliated.

'What d'you mean by giving us a bloody fright like that?' Frank tried to recover a few vestiges of self-respect by attack but Ben came back with counter attack.

'Look, you don't think I enjoy slamming into crates and stumbling round this hell hole in the middle of the night during a storm, do you?'

'Who's asking you to?'

'Hey, what sort of welcome is this, anyway? God knows I've had a tough time trying to track you lot down. I saw you and your crazy old Moggie down at Kippford, when we were filming ghastly Gavin and his grey shirts the other day. Could have sworn *you* saw *me*.' He sounded aggrieved.

'Pull up some dirt and sit down.' Frank, I remembered, had been very well brought up.

'I don't think so. I thought it'd be great with you coming up here and me working on assignments in the area'…. Which no doubt he'd contrived, I thought. ' I imagined we'd all get together like old times. Remember those marvellous holidays we had?'

We managed not to groan – just. He was pathetic – trawling round after us and now he was about to trash the last day of our holiday.

'…. And when R. C. Erskine mentioned this project, it was even more imperative to chase you up. Wouldn't have found you now, if it hadn't been for Dunc.'

'Dunc?'

'Duncan from The Grannoch. I called in this evening. I may use him for a spot of local colour and literary associations – and he mentioned this property... some yarn about Mary Queen of Scots.'

'And?'

'He said, funnily enough three guys with an old Morris Minor had expressed interest in the house only today – maybe even thought of camping there. And so...'

'So, here you are'

'Right'

'So now?'

'So now we can all enjoy ourselves together. I'm free tomorrow and we should...'

'Look, shut up a minute... have a drink.... We may already have made plans.'

Ben's torch was one of those smart ones that turns into a lamp when you pull it upwards. He was holding it aloft and I wondered if he registered the despondency on our illuminated faces. It wouldn't have meant anything to him if he *had*. He was definitely one up and we were ninety-nine down.

'Oh, I think we can do better than this' he said, as Frank held out a red plastic mug. 'I've got sole use of Erskin's Merc – it's outside. (By the way, thanks for leaving all the gates open) And not only his car but his house: he had to fly up to Edinburgh on Thursday. It's an unprepossessing place but suits me well enough while we're filming up here. But that,' he held the lamp up to my face at this point 'is the sad, sad thing. He flew back to London this afternoon.'

'Well, I don't think I'll lose any sleep over it. I've never met him. Who is he anyway?' I asked.

'Who is he?'

Rex answered. 'R. C. Erskine – big, big boss of Olympia Television – among other things.'

'So?' I couldn't see where this was leading.

'It's sad for both of us really' Ben continued in this melancholy manner. 'He has a passion for the area – brought up here.. endearing childhood memories and all that. He had the idea of this series of programmes – aspects of Galloway, encouraged by me – I've had a lot of input in all this, I may say. I've got R.C.s' ear in most things.'

'Crawler' I was thinking.

'He's just bought this house Glen Stramon, *not* house beautiful, bit grim, run down – though not quite in this league.' He looked round briefly. 'Anyway, he plans to do it up. Has a thing about Charles Rennie McIndoe.

'Mackintosh' I corrected him, feeling my pulse rate quickening.

'Yes, him. I told R.C. I know just the architect – great friend of mine – you. Job like that would be worth a bomb – total makeover. I even rang your mother-in-law – really tried. I wanted to set up a meeting while he was here. He was keen…. But….' He shrugged… 'End of story.'

Oh my God, oh my God, oh my God. A commission to die for… to live for…. Pure pleasure…. The publicity…. The contacts…. The money…..

' He's an impatient guy. When he wants a job done, he wants it done yesterday and it isn't as if he wont know plenty of other architects, or architectural consultants or designers or other...'

'Fringe phonies' I growled furiously. Here we'd been, fooling around with this childish cat and mouse game, ducking and dodging and all the time..... I wondered for a second if it was all on the level – could this be his idea of revenge for something? But then he said.

'To be honest, the whole enterprise could have done *me* no harm at all. If you glue yourself to the shirt tails of someone like R.C., the sky's the limit. I mean, I don't intend to end up doing these feature programmes – no way! I want my own chat show.'

This was more like it – a favour not only for me but for himself – of course I could see his point – so 'Thanks anyway' I managed.

'Tough luck' Frank said to me as if I'd been bowled out in a school match. Rex said 'I know just how you feel.' But how could either realise the enormity of this lost opportunity?

'Let's get out of this rubbish tip before we're kippered' Ben suggested 'What brought you here anyway, for God's sake?'

'Rex's putting in an offer.'

'No kidding!.'

* * *

TWENTY THREE

The fire had petered out so, stiff and stinking, we all climbed through the window and made a dash for the Mercedes which enfolded us in sybaritic excess. Hedonists at heart, we threw off the simple life with no trouble at all and gave in to its customised comforts – the drinks cabinet opening up behind the front seat, the music (we had cool jazz for wild cats through the night) the leg room, reclining seats...

'I got Dunc to put me up some sandwiches. Want one? Cheese – Lockerbie Cheddar – I've got a taste for it. I wonder if there's a Lockerbie Wensleydale...'

'Thanks' Frank's hand shot out.

'How's Jane and the infant Olivia?' Ben asked. He was always good on names and that sort of stuff.

I explained where they were and that they should be on their PAN AM way to Argentina now.

Bits of sandwich shot out of Rex's mouth as he squawked 'There you go again! I've told you that word's out of bounds and you just keep going on and on about it, don't you? What is it with you?'

'You're crazy.'

'What word's that?' Ben swivelled round from the front seat.

'Panama, as he very well knows.' Black looks directed at me.

'Panama, Panama' Ben said thoughtfully, living dangerously. He produced a newspaper from a door pocket and unfolded it, turning to the financial section.

'Like to keep track of my stocks and shares – get some hot tips now and then from my cousin Serena. Very astute girl that: she's doing a line with a bloke, Con, who works for Crass Dippy and keeps his ear to the ground. As a matter of fact, he's somewhere around at the moment – they're doing one of those awful building-cardboard-bridges-over-the-Bering-Straits sort of thing. A friend of his father's throwing a party at his place tomorrow and Serena's coming up for it. She said I could tag along.'

Rex was breathing fire now, what with 'Panama' being bandied about coupled with the name of his old flame, and Ben heard him.

'Oops, I was forgetting. You know Serena, of course. You and she… Well, entre nous, I hear on the grape vine… well, the horse's mouth, actually, that things aren't too rosy with her and Con just at present– so you could be in there. What was I looking for? Oh yes, here it is – headline: -

'Panamanian Continental Highway Bonds Soar.'

'Give me that!' Rex snatched at the paper rudely: I remembered he had not been very well brought up. He read out

'The revolution in Panama which has caused instability in these bonds over the last few days, has been crushed. A new regime is emerging which will restore confidence to the market. Yes!' He ruffled Ben's yellow hair, let out a wild, ecstatic whoop, opened the car door and leapt out into the rain and wind and wasn't seen for at least three minutes.

'What was all that about?' Ben asked him when he returned, wet and no less wild. And we heard.

As fund manager for his hugely thrusting City Merchant Bank, he'd taken a mega risk recently, investing in Bonds which had plummeted and risen, dipped and ascended in an uneasy pattern mirrored, I saw now, in Rex's moods.

He'd bottled all this up. Well, I'd bottled up St Ethel's and what was Jane up to, I'd like to know?

Anyway, Rex was happy, Frank was happy – he had food and Ben was now Mr Tolerable, Mr Fair to Middling.

'So… what shall we do tomorrow?' Ben asked – one of the gang now, like everyone's best friend.

'We've got to get the keys back to the estate agents, clock in to our hotel, get some breakfast, clear up the mess here…' Frank said.

'Mmmm, sounds like a load of fun. But no can do' Ben said quickly. 'As a matter of fact, I've just remembered there's someone I want to interview for a feature I'm doing on Buchan – 39 Steps Through Galloway. Her great grandfather used to fish with him. I could fit it in in the morning. She was telling me that J.B. stayed once or twice at Stewartston, where I'm partying tomorrow: he knew the family. Terrific old place, apparently, probably worth a programme on its own.

I was sinking into a sleepy stupor, but became aware of Frank's and Rex's (more) animated voices.

'Reels at Stewartston. That's bloody marvellous – we're going to be there too.'

So Rex could be happy on two counts. Panama and a chance to score with Serena.

'Fantastic. How come?' Ben asked, so Frank explained vaguely about the Tattie connection.

'And did I hear you mention hotel? Forget it. Come and share the hospitality of the absent R.C. Plenty of room' Ben offered with largesse.

But we already planned to gate crash the party and Frank, remembering he was well brought up, drew the line at staying uninvited at someone's house in their absence. 'Thanks but no thanks – bit late to unscramble our arrangements.'

I was in two minds about this. Part of me would have been professionally intrigued to see the house but another part felt the misery of what might have been. Moody blues. Jazz turned low. The smoke from Rex's cigarette swirled round and I nodded off to Bix Beiderbeck and Frank's pleased chat with Ben about what shape the Buchan programme might take.

* * *

TWENTY FOUR

I noticed that Ben opened all the car doors wide after we'd got out – act of fumigation, I supposed.

We stretched and did some halfhearted runnings on the spot, and prepared to gather up the sad remains of our camping.

'The weather was against us' Frank said, yawning. There was no question of shaving – no-one could be bothered at this stage to collect water (nothing to collect it in, anyway) or boil it up (our pan was wrecked). Electric razors had been left at home as part of Frank's plan for simple living.

'Well, I'll be off, then. Tell you what – come over to Glen Stramon for a drink. Party doesn't start till 9.30 and Serena said be sure to have a reels practice beforehand. Vital, apparently. Oh and bound to be black tie. See you about 7.30 – cheers!' and Ben was of with a screech of tyres, which made a contribution to the already considerable number of ruts in the drive.

'Did he say black tie? Frank asked gloomily,

watching the Mercedes speed towards the gates and vanish round a corner flanked by giant rhododendrons.

'Oh, anything goes nowadays.' Nothing was going to deflect Rex from his big night out.

'And, anyway, we could always buy three bow ties when we take the keys back.' I wasn't sure how ties would match up with grungy T-shirts and filthy jeans to give the required formality. Not even Frank's tweed jacket would fit the bill.

'So, you've decided to join us, have you? Frank asked me and I said 'Definitely maybe and maybe definitely' and he took this as 'Yes.'

'Good.'

We found a packet of oatcakes in the tent, which was now flapping dismally in the breeze. More rips had appeared in the side.

'Definitely not worth packing up and taking back' Rex said 'We could chuck it in the first tip we see.'

'D'you realise – my father used this tent when he was a boy!' Frank yelled and gathered it up tenderly and back it went on to the roof rack.

The wind and returning sun and warmth soon dried up most signs of the previous night's rain and the grounds became a virgin paradise once more. The chimneys on the house were intact and the little burn was babbling and sparkling. I splashed the cool water over my face and drank some to get rid of the dusty dryness of several oatcakes.

'It's a great place' Frank said wistfully 'I really think I…'

'Steady,' I warned: he just smiled.

* * *

The key worked for us this time so we made our entrance through the front door into the hall. I don't think our time there had made it look any worse than it had looked before. We picked up the still damp sleeping bags and collected the gas ring, but drew the line at the pan. We didn't want it, with its unappealing remains and evidence of the said haggis abuse, so we left it and it looked quite at home amongst the wreckage.

* * *

'So…. What did you think? Are you interested?' Liz Chase had to reach a long way forward for the keys which Frank handed to her. He was sitting at a small table opposite her and I'd noticed that she'd scraped her chair back as far as it would go as we'd approached as if we were a threat in some way. But she managed to keep a smile pinned on her face – just. Then she took a hanky out from a sleeve, blew her nose gently and kept the hanky in place.

Rex, not wanting to risk catching a cold, said he'd wait outside.

'I had a thorough inspection with my architect.' Frank was being all business like. 'It's a very interesting property… and I've decided….'

Liz Chase raised her eyebrows encouragingly.

'Definitely maybe.'

I didn't know whether to take this for 'yes.'

He asked if he could take particulars of other properties and she quickly sorted out a large pile in the preferred price range and locations, gave him her Agent's mag. and opened the door for us – not closing it behind us.

'Breakfast!'

'Elevenses.' I said, hearing a church clock chime. I asked Rex if he wanted that dental appointment but –

' No, the tooth's switched off, thank God.' Stunned by the continued rush of adrenalin and whisky last night, I supposed.

We grabbed filled rolls and cartons of coffee before heading off towards Castle Douglas to book in at the Gordon Arms. I was beginning to think of home and the pleasure of regular meals, and planned a shower and an afternoon spent prone on my bed with eyes tight shut.

'Needs to talk to you' still niggled uncomfortably. No good ringing Anna's – Jane and Livvie (and Chris?) should be on their way to South America now. Useless to ring Jane's mother and alarm her.

About five miles before the town, as we were driving along, we spotted a small country show taking place in a fold of the hills. Tents had been set up, railings for stock– and riders and ponies were trotting around. The whole scene was so enticing, so gentle, soothing to the senses and so timeless that we all, even Rex who was still in good humour, remarked on it.

'That's a must for this afternoon' Frank said.

Bang went my date with my bed but I agreed, it was too good to miss and I could always have a snooze behind the largest marrow.

The Gordon Arms was a pleasant, solid hotel of the late Georgian period but there was obviously a whiff of sulphur about us – or maybe it was soot– which gave offence as the receptionist drew back while we signed the register.

We asked for a late key, not knowing what time we'd be back from the party and her attitude changed the moment we mentioned reels at Stewartston. She tried a smile. Stewartston was obviously a magic word locally … The Big Hoose.

'That'll be just fine.'

Our rooms wouldn't be ready till twelve o'clock so we went to do some shopping. Rex said he needed a new (black) shirt and I was commissioned to buy three bow ties.

We'd meet later and go to the Show mid afternoon.

I knew where Frank would be going and I was right. I saw him vanish into Williamson's estate agents for his regular fix of particulars.

Feeling I'd be bounced out of any gathering, however informal, with my present wardrobe, I bought a shirt (green). Jane hates the colour but I was feeling revengeful for something, though I wasn't sure what. I also bought three bow ties (tartan), which I thought looked striking.

We met up at three and found our way back to the Glens Country Show and parked. It looked just as inviting as it had in the morning. More crowded now but it looked a cheerful crowd, relaxed in the sun, which glinted on parked cars, harnesses and horse shoes, the latter being hurled towards a metal peg with varying degrees of success by sturdy youths to cries of encouragement. It was hard to avoid being trampled on by frisky ponies, swerving, cantering, bucking, hardly curbed by their young and very young riders.

The muffled words over the loud speaker were unintelligible but it didn't seem to matter. People surrounding the show ring were going to enjoy whatever event came next, be it knife throwing or guessing the weight of the organiser. Small marquees housing crafts, floral arrangements, homemade cakes, flapped in the warm breeze and we couldn't wait to be part of it all.

* * *

TWENTY FIVE

Surrounding the show ground were stalls selling everything you could need for setting up as a countryman, including one selling second hand books and a selection of adult looking videos– to while away the long winter nights perhaps.

After we'd had some of the best ice creams we'd ever tasted, Frank made a beeline for a country wear stall. He felt the need, he said, for a pair of green wellies.

As he slipped his wide feet into them, he uttered a sigh of contentment as if he'd been on a long, tedious journey and had now come home. He kept them on and reached out for a plastic bag containing his old shoes, bumping heads as he did so with a tall, healthy looking young woman who was reaching out at the same second for another pair of green wellies. Apologies and smiles. Frank looked after her as she walked towards ponies and riders novelty sack race and then sauntered off in the direction of 'Home Made Produce.' Rex had disappeared.

I leant up against a tree and decided to try to capture the essence of this rustic idyll…. the refreshing innocence that is not much apparent in N.W.1. these days. Soft blue hills surrounded the little show in a protective corral with the movement, activity and colourful stalls held within like a vivid kaleidoscope. Difficult to reproduce in a quick watercolour but not impossible.

Soft accents of three farmers nearby, having a group grizzle about the weather – not nearly enough rain the night before– were soothing: they moved off.

Looking up at one point, I noticed without really noticing that a hefty bull was making its own peaceful way over towards me, not being led, nor causing any nuisance to anybody it stared with a stern but friendly avuncular gaze and came to a full stop just a few yards away. This did not bother me at all – after all, no-one was chasing after it: everyone was far too busy watching the Young Farmers 'hurl the wellie' or inspecting close curled ochre-coloured sheep being judged near the dog show. He was obviously one of the afternoon's attractions, I thought, giving rides to children instead of a donkey… or 'guess his nickname' or number of progeny' and we looked at each other in a restful, pleasant way. He was saying 'Isn't all this delightful?' and 'Am I going to be in your picture?' and 'I've just got to go and check something then I'll come back and pose for you.' He lumbered off into an adjacent empty pen and, just in case I'd got it all completely wrong, I closed it.

It turned out his name was Jericho – famous in two counties for his fury and fighting spirit.

I had a brief moment of fame when the owner,

shaken, realised what had happened and thumped me on the back by way of thanks reviving himself with swigs from his hip flask while others nearby nodded approval.

Having no hip flask, I felt a strong cup of tea might be the next but three best thing and found the refreshment tent. Tattie, wearing a large blue rain hat, and au pair Jutte were at the head of the queue as I joined it, and staggering around with a tray of empties was my dancing partner of the Barreough. She spotted me, dumped her load on a table and her 'Och, it's guid to see you – how about another wee cha, cha, eh?' made everyone turn their heads. She laughed and wriggled her hips.

Huge embarrassment. I glanced at Tattie but of course she hadn't recognised me.

Rex, I soon discovered had found a stall selling nothing but whisky liqueurs and offering free samples; he'd spent a happy time comparing and contrasting.

'And what d' you think of this?' he asked and pulled from a carrier bag – a panama. He gave a wry smile. To make some sort of statement, I supposed.

'Put it on.'

He did and looked strangely exotic. But not more so than a popular figure hailed as Guysie, selling beads and flapjacks under a banner which read 'Poppies and Moons – everything Organic.'

Ragged children with unkempt hair danced round us – obviously taking us for one of their own and a couple of mongrel dogs growled. An attractive young woman with a dirty face breast-fed twins, unconcerned that she was proving a bigger attraction to the Young Farmers than the display of tractors nearby.

'Guysie' seemed to know everyone and everyone seemed to know him and greeted him warmly, not put off by greasy, Fagin locks and filthy long fingernails which rummaged around in beans and lentils. Tattie wandered over to speak to him.

Music, coming over the loud speakers, was suddenly snapped off and an incomprehensibly muffled announcement was made which no-one understood but, referring to their programmes, people made their way to the main ring to watch a Tug of War between the Animal Rights Liberation Group and Field Sports Society and we caught up with Frank. We weren't sure it was him at first – with a new tweed hat pulled well down, a new 'all weather' waistcoat, his new green wellies and carrying brand new fishing rod and a knobbly walking stick, he blended effortlessly into his surroundings.

But when he shouted to us we knew it was him. He drew out from a pocket, a red and white spotted snuff handkerchief I hadn't seen before and mopped his brow. 'God, it's hot.'

The tug of war contestants looked hot too and the crowd became partisan cheering or jeering. A particularly robust guy in the front line of Animal Rights lost his balance and fell heavily, squashing a Cairn terrier which yelped piteously, causing angry mutters and withdrawal of support.

Frank had come across Jock, taking half an hour off to visit the show before taking a party stalking: he'd given Frank help over choosing some fishing tackle.

'That'll be handy on Highgate Ponds' Rex said, looking at the rod. I was only idly following their talk. I was thinking how bizarre to come hundreds of miles from home, go to an event and know at least three people there after only a few days, whereas you'd go grey and toothless before getting so much as a friendly nod from someone across the street at home.

The tug of war ended in a draw as both teams collapsed in a sweaty heap with cheers exceeding jeers: queues outside the beer tent were soon forming. Frank didn't do queues. He jerked his head in the direction of the car park and raised an eyebrow under the shadow of the tweedy brim. We got the message and the answer was a big fat 'yes.' I was yawning and Rex looked as if he was sleep walking. The thought of a heavy night ahead spent partying was unimaginable.

Nodding off on our way back to the Gordon Arms, I heard Frank murmur in a satisfied and contented way about the afternoon's activities... the sunny weather... the sunny atmosphere. I agreed. There may have been rumbles of dissention rolling beneath the surface and there were opportunities enough – malicious mums, bad tempered ponies, despised dogs, rejected produce and suspect partisan judges, but if there were we'd been unaware of it, totally unaffected; it had all passed over our heads.

* * *

It was just as well we'd booked an alarm call for 6 o'clock as I'd fallen into a heavy sleep. We met up in the lounge and looked at each other, with our tartan bow ties; we resembled a sad old-time music hall act.

We looked in no way formal and I believe even Frank had minor misgivings but managed an 'O.k. – fine. Now food. I can't dance on an empty stomach.'

'And I, sure as hell, can't dance on a full one' I said.

Rex said he'd settle for a double espresso – in fact he claimed he needed at least three after an afternoon of serious liqueur sampling.

In any event, we were too early for dinner and afternoon teas were finished. There were high teas from six o'clock, we were told, but these were just for children. Frank suggested they were being ageist and he'd be perfectly happy with a substantial high tea.

I don't think we'd have been allowed to join the half dozen or so under tens at a long table in the otherwise deserted dining room, if Frank hadn't remembered to utter the magic word 'Stewartston', but he did, and we sat there eating our chicken nuggets and fish fingers with baked beans, all of us swapping corny jokes with the kids and trying to store up the best ones.

* * *

I dreaded seeing Glen Stramon. I knew that whatever it looked like, my imagination would shift into over drive and I'd be planning, feverishly, fantastic designs for its transformation into an inspirational pastiche of a Charles Rennie Mackintosh house. Research would have been pure pleasure, browsing through my extensive collection of books on the subject and immersing myself in the style and aesthetic flair of the man.

Rex, in the front of the car, was looking out for road

signs. 'I bumped into that au pair of Tattie's at the Show…. Jutta – she kept following me around.' (He didn't sound as if he'd minded this.) 'She said she'd been made to practise reels every evening "Very difficult," she said.'

'I glimpsed Tattie in the Refreshment Tent after the incident with the bull' I said but they showed no interest in the bull. Frank swore softly.

'Why the hell didn't you ask her about the dress code?'

I pointed out that it wouldn't have made much difference what the dress code was, our sartorial choice being strictly limited.

* * *

TWENTY SIX

The house looked as if it had been purpose built in the 1920s as a reformatory or, at best, Glen Stramon Research Institute. The plain façade was completely characterless – dull brick and mean windows – but, as such, offered exciting scope for enhancement. I tried to think of something else but it was difficult.

Ben appeared at the boring front door in the guise of genial host, looking like someone AWOL from the cast of Rob Roy. His tartan trews were of such a dazzling variety of colours that Rex rummaged for his raybans. He wore a velvet jacket over a white shirt with lace ruffles at the neck and cuff. He looked pleased at our stares of incredulity.

'My middle name's Chatten' he said as if this explained something.

Rex, not to be outdone, struck an attitude. 'And are we dead cool, or what?'

'Do those bow ties of yours whirl round when you

press a button?' he just asked and led the way indoors as a white van vanished down the drive.

'We've had the electricians in doing some work' (We, *we*?) 'There's going to be an upstairs cinema – necessary in our line of work – among other things. Come and have a drink.'

He was not only a genial host but a lavish one and produced a couple of bottles of fine wine 'from R.C.'s collection of Vintage Claret' kept in the cellar ' and there's more where that came from.'

The rooms matched the exterior in blandness but were overlaid in my eyes with striking simplicity and subtle coloured highlights. I took a long drink. Oh, the piquant hell of what might have been.

Ben was half way to promising an enthusiastic Frank a two minute slot, on his John Buchan programme – concerning the food preferences of Richard Hannay. The two were in a huddle.

'Look – how about this reels practice?' Rex lit a cigarette and inhaled deeply. Jutta's words had got to him.

'Go and see what you can find in the way of music – over there.' Ben nodded towards a cabinet.

R.C.'s taste in music was Catholic but the only patriotic C.D. we could find was 'Laments of the Islands' played by the pipes of a Highland Division. We put it on but it depressed our spirits so much that we had no inclination to dance and could only stare mournfully and shake our heads. 'Besides,' Frank pointed out, 'the rhythm was all wrong' and we'd have to sing or hum.

'How do we go about the business? Where's the

book of instructions?' Rex asked reasonably and we all looked at Ben.

'Well, don't look at me. I thought perhaps Frank….'

'I think I remember doing an Eightsome some years ago.' He thought back 'It involved a circle with someone prancing about in the middle of it.'

'Well, we could try that' and Rex stubbed out his cigarette, held out his hands and Ben and I joined up to form a tight circle, Frank squeezed into the centre and executed some fancy footwork with some panache. We did this for a few minutes while we each sang or hummed our own versions of something light hearted.

'That was all right – what next?'

Frank searched back into his past 'There was something called a chain, some people went one way and some the other, grabbing hands.'

It took us some while to get the hang of this despite Frank's graphic description but with alternate hands coming at you as you went round in a circle we worked up such a speed that we became dizzy and fell down.

'Don't think we'll have any problem with that one' Rex said confidently picking up small tables, an ash tray and glasses we'd knocked over.

'What about that Crashing White Sergeant we tried at the Barreough?' I said, not really wanting to remind myself of that evening but feeling that just one perfected reel might not be enough.

'I know that dance' Ben said, 'at least I know the name but we need partners, don't we?'

R.Cs two Burmese cats, Zeus and Juno sat on a sofa, looking at us sardonically.

'Cushions and bottles' suggested Rex.

We pooled our scant knowledge.

'We were in threes' Frank said.

So Rex and I chose a plump red cushion as our bonnie lasses and Frank and Ben went for lean and mean – a bottle of Chablis each.

We decided that we'd all hum the same tune this time and settled on Auld Lang Syne.

'Circles and lines and sort of weaving in and out' I said optimistically. We weaved and hummed but our 'women' obstructed us, getting in our way at every turn, mine infuriating me so much that I whirled 'her' round my head, flung 'her' to the ground and jumped on 'her.' We'd started our song on too high a note and couldn't keep it up so continued in a grim silence.

Anyone watching from outside might have thought we were taking part in a satanic ritual.

I think the dance was meant to be a fun thing, remembering the shrieks of laughter at the Barreough, and Rex did try to get into the spirit of the thing with much toe pointing that was quite pretty to watch, but there was a cheerlessness about the whole thing and when Ben's wino women keeled over and rolled away, he said irritably 'Enough's bloody well enough.'

'Well, I think we got that sorted o.k. Shouldn't have any problems there' Frank said happily. The rest of us lacked his certainty. 'Serena will kill me,' Ben muttered. 'You know what she's like.' We all knew what Ben's cousin was like. Rex looked worried and lit another cigarette.

I wanted to cool down after all the activity but Ben

raised the frill round his wrist and looked at his Rolex. 'Good Lord – is that the time – we'd better be moving.' His eye flickered over us briefly 'Look, you push off. I've got to put the cats out, lock up. We'll go separately – we'll meet up there, right?'

Right. He was ashamed of us. Didn't want to be seen going in with three deadbeats like us. Funny that. He'd try and avoid us after *we'd* been at pains to avoid him for days.

He gave us directions to Stewartston. 'Grounds run down to the coast. They own hundreds of acres, thousands probably, farms, saw mills, you name it and the house is fantastic – bags of atmosphere – anyway, you'll see for yourselves.'

So, we were to be gate crashing on our own. Wouldn't even have the dubious connection of Ben, cousin of Serena, who was (just about) ex girl friend of Con, whose father was a friend of the host. Gate crashers, like teenagers doing it for a bet.

We roared down the empty, darkening roads at a steady 40 m.p.h. and of course, were soon overtaken by the Mercedes. Ben trying to be incognito didn't toot.

We took a turning signed 'Stewartston' hoping to discover the drive and main gates but the road continued and after about three miles through farmland and park, sighting a tantalising glimpse of a tower house over trees, we realised that the road *was* the drive.

Cars were parked to no particular plan in a field and we pulled up alongside a four-wheel drive. Another car came up behind and from its headlights we saw the Merc. Parked at right angles to everyone else.

From the field we emerged through a belt of tall trees on to a gravelly path and I stood stock still, overwhelmed by the grandeur and antiquity of a huge tower house, illuminated by a discreet floodlight. That was not all: it was attached to a magnificent Georgian Chapel towering above us now, the ecclesiastical stained glass windows lit up from inside. The whole effect was thrilling and dramatic and I fiddled in my pocket for my sketchbook,

'What the hell are you doing?' Frank asked. 'Listen, I've got a cunning plan. Follow me.'

I guessed at a Georgian wing round the corner and possibly earlier extensions linking the whole and promised myself that at some stage during the evening I'd get lost.

Frank led the way through a stone arch and into a courtyard, following small flares stuck in the ground guiding our way to a door.

Frank's plan was to hide in the adjacent overgrown shrubbery, until a group of partygoers appeared then attach ourselves to them and mingle and continue to mingle until we were absorbed and just hope our host wouldn't be counting.

'Simple as all the best schemes' and Frank took up a position beside some laurels.

There was a light shining out from the door, which I guessed was the old kitchen entrance, and we could see a couple of people silhouetted against it: we could also see the figure of a man as he emerged from behind a large shrub. He was coming over towards us. He spoke 'That you Frank? Just tidying myself up – look, we could go in together.'

Ben's white shirt dazzled but was now open at the neck, the sleeves rolled up and he carried his velvet jacket over one arm. Then I knew why. A group of laughing, chattering revellers, already wined and dined, were making their way towards the house. Dress code? Casual, relaxed, even wacky.

* * *

TWENTY SEVEN

We pushed and shoved our way in as members of an animated gang. As I squeezed alongside a girl with a bare, chubby midriff, she smiled and her raised eyebrow said 'Do I know you?' but that was all. No sentry on guard or anyone asking to see tickets. We were in! and propelled along a narrow, low ceilinged corridor, up a flight of oak stairs and into a scrum culminating in a little room on the right, where people were helping themselves to drinks and shouting at the tops of their voices. Even Frank had a job making himself heard and had to sign something to me, though I couldn't make out the meaning of his wild theatrical gestures.

We'd lost Rex altogether and I suppose Ben had gone to hunt down Serena.

I managed eventually to reach out an arm through the throng and establish a glass of my own into which I poured whisky and lemonade and was about to try picking it up without being jostled when suddenly there was a blast of music from beyond followed by silence. I was nearly knocked over as everyone surged towards the door and then I was on my own.

Picking up my drink, I followed the crowd through an archway and found myself in a small gallery with stairs leading down to a large chapel with high vaulted ceiling, empty of pews and with huge arched windows. One or two small religious statues stood in alcoves, surveying the secular scene with forbearance.

Someone called out 'Take your partners for Hamilton House and the buzz rose to fever pitch as people sorted themselves out into pairs. I thought I was safe, aloof in the gallery, but not a bit of it. I was seized enthusiastically by a strong hand.

'I recognise *you*. You were at the Show and saved us all from being gored by that frightful bull!' I looked down into a pair of laughing blue eyes belonging to a young woman who looked a bit like Jane. 'Good God' she went on 'we could all have been killed – you're a hero!' This was beguiling stuff.

'Well, he was really…' I began modestly.

'Come on – it's my favourite reel – we can join on the end here' and she pulled me, dragged me, on to the floor.

My knowledge of the two dances we'd practised was scanty – the memory of them fading fast and Hamilton House I'd never heard of. She saw the panic in my eyes.

'It's easy – you'll be fine. It's sometimes called The Flirters' Reel,' she shouted.

None of this reassured me. 'Flirters' Reel' – what was expected of me? Should I wink?

We were on the end of a long line of happy laughing people, partners facing each other.

'Don't worry! The music will tell you what to do!' she yelled.

The music started coming via wires draped over hymn number boards, cones and a couple of deeply religious paintings and led to a music centre, standing by a stone font, and amplifiers – it came loud and strong but told me nothing. I had a quick look at the two other long lines but no sign of Frank or Rex – crafty devils. I was reeling in panic.

'Watch the others!' she yelled again.

I was standing next to a boy of about ten who seemed to be partnering his grandmother. He was probably new to the game too. I gave him a conspiratorial nudge. 'We'll just give it our best shot, eh?' He nodded pleasantly and turned his attention back to the activity which had moved up the line and was now perilously close. The young boy whirled his grandmother expertly. He was in total command and suddenly gave me a prod and a frown. I was meant to be doing something, but what? I had no time to wonder as I was seized roughly, twirled then abandoned, then shoved and pushed unceremoniously into different positions, slipping on the French chalk, giving my partner a sharp, accidental kick on the ankle and finishing up in a frenzied circle. I thought that was it but no, I swear the whole thing went on for forty minutes and I finished up bruised and humiliated. My partner's laughing eyes had turned sad. I thanked her and slunk away as she joined some friends. How come it had been so impossibly difficult? It seemed to require just a few basic movements – a child of about ten could do it! I caught sight of Rex leaning over the gallery looking at me with an amused expression, so I had a sharp word with him before going to get a drink, then spotted a vacant chair at the side down in the main body of the chapel where I could sit in peace and perhaps do a quick pencil sketch. Before I reached it, though, to my surprise I was hailed by my ex-reels partner and she beckoned me over to join her and a couple of girl friends. She was friendly again, my disgrace forgotten.

'Who's the good looking guy in black? Is he famous? I noticed you spoke to him.'

She was looking up at the gallery and it was Rex they were all looking at. He was now the centre of some attention – the sleek blackbird again preening himself. I hadn't known who he'd been looking forward to seeing most at the party –

Issy (who'd been at Tattie's for drinks)– maybe

Jutta – probably not

Serena – probably

The three were now gathered round him, Serena looking gorgeous in scarlet and while we looked they were joined by Courtney of Crass Dippy, team mate of Con, Serena's sometime boyfriend.

'He looks vaguely familiar'

'Opera' I said

'Mmm, yes, he has that haunted look. Operas are *so* not happy – they always end in a wail.'

She was right, he did look haunted. His circle of admirers had increased by another – this time it was Flora from the Grannoch who'd spotted him. I remembered she'd said her boyfriend's (uncle?) was hosting a party and this was it. Of the boyfriend there was no sign, fishing still perhaps.

Then – 'The next dance will be a Dashing White Sergeant', and people began to cluster together and organise threesomes.

I glanced up at Rex, interested to know how he'd sort this one out. The look of desperation on his face made me feel quite sorry for him for a brief moment and then, as I looked, a transformation came over him. He gazed out over the chapel and the people thronging below and was staring at a fixed point to my right. Turning, I saw the object of his attention was the woman he'd met on our first day in Scotland at Caerlaverock. The one who'd recognised the piece he'd been whistling and from whom I'd ruthlessly torn him away. Alice Van something. She had seen him too and I could feel the crackle of electricity pass between them. Then like in an old black and white B movie, they moved towards each other – it seemed in slow motion –oblivious of everyone around them.

I didn't notice what happened to his harem as at that moment the familiar opening chord of music came as a warning and simultaneously I was seized by Tattie wearing something pale and floaty and Frank to make up a three for the reel.

I had planned to lose myself in some quiet corner or start my secret inspection of the house but Frank shouted 'We practised this, remember! Lines, weaving and passing under arches' he said unhelpfully. Under Tattie's guidance, we eventually got the hang of it and felt ridiculously pleased with ourselves, although Frank confessed afterwards he'd found it easier with bottles and cushions. He said his old leg wound acquired at Dirk Hattrick's cave was playing up a bit and he wasn't sure if he'd be able to manage any more dancing.

'Come and say hello to Lulu' Tattie said to him 'she's just arrived back from Peru. She's finding something to eat in the kitchen.' This sounded like good news to Frank and I tagged along anxious to start my private tour.

'Didn't you do something frightfully brave with a bull this afternoon?' she asked me. News travels fast.

Back down the corridor we went, catching tantalising glimpses of snug panelled rooms, a cosy library, other softly lit corridors, leading away to the Georgian wing? The Tower?

The kitchen table was piled with plates, cutlery, and a generous amount of food: large quiches, cold chicken, salads jostled for space with fruitcakes, fruit pies and cheeses and there were only four or five others helping themselves. Tattie's daughter was not among them but I recognised someone I'd seen at the Show – the man they called Guysie. He had not scrubbed up well. His kilt must have seen in a hundred Hogmanays, been danced on vigorously, left out in the rain frequently and used as a doormat. It was difficult to see where his hair ended and his beard began such was the tangle – an earring glinted through the coils but Tattie looked at him fondly and introduced us to him. 'Francis – son of an old school friend and… er…'

I told her my name but she got it wrong.

'Guy Lauriston-Laurie. Guysie sometimes comes

back to see us from his commune up in the hills, don't you? They share everything up there.' This to Frank. 'Even their womenfolk, rumour has it,' she added naughtily and gave her tinkling laugh. But Guy ignored it and went on chewing away at a hunk of game pie, the pastry crumbs of which had met up with globules of chutney in his beard and were doing a little dance.

'What news of the big hoose?' she asked Guy 'Any buyers?' He just shrugged and she turned to Frank, who was piling food on to his plate. 'My mother remembered wonderful parties at Knocksting in the old days.' Frank stopped cutting a generous portion of the game pie and turned to her. Of course, of *course*, Guy owned the ruined Upper Knocksting.

'I must go and find Gavin.' Tattie was getting no mileage from Guy.

'Anyway, where's Lulu got to?' She grabbed a sausage roll and floated away.

I took the piece of game pie that Frank had been cutting, wrapped it in a napkin and left, Frank opening his mouth to say something to Guy. I hoped he wouldn't say something silly like 'I'll make you an offer for the place.'

I was free to explore. I'd say I was looking for the cloakroom if anyone was interested.

The room next to the kitchen was a low ceilinged dining room – oak furniture, Turkish rugs, military portraits and battle scenes now being glanced at vaguely by Tattie's son Sandy. He was balancing a drink and a plate full of cocktail sausages and fruitcake in one hand while the other held a drink for Tattie's aunt, while she sorted out her dog, who had cocked his leg on one of the chairs. Tattie, who appeared from a group of friends, did some mopping up with paper napkins and I stood aside while Hurricane Serena suddenly burst in looking dangerous.

'Where's that bastard Rex?' she asked me. I suppose she half remembered me from the old days. 'He just...' Her face was white, her slanting eyes furious, she was not used to being rebuffed. Those beautiful wicked eyes came to rest on Sandy. She was in the mood to enslave someone else. She looked at him, his eyes clicked into focus for the first time and he was lost.

'Oh, there you are, Serena.' Ben stood in the door. 'They're doing the Reel of the 51st Division next, interested?' But Serena's eyes were locked with Sandy's: He looked as if he'd mislaid his script but just about managed to say 'May I have this dance?'

Tattie looked up from her mopping as they left. Serena – army wife material? I didn't think so but it was none of my business.

Ben said 'Have I missed something?'

'Not really.'

'Did you say Reel of the 51st?' Tattie's aunt shrieked. 'It's my absolute favourite.' She pushed Pong Poo into the arms of a tall handsome girl standing nearby, who looked familiar. 'Here, Lulu, look after him for me' and flinging aside her walking stick impatiently, she seized Ben and limped off with him down the corridor.

* * *

TWENTY EIGHT

Taking a bite of game pie, I looked into the room opposite and saw Gavin in his signature grey, asleep with his mouth open as if about to give a command. In repose, he looked cross and not relaxed. This was the library, untidy, with some very old plaster work and an interesting carved mantelpiece and I wanted to have the room to myself to enjoy its atmosphere and study it properly. But the old door had creaked as I'd opened it wider and Gavin twitched violently and opened his eyes.

I had an idea, in fact I had two.

'Food is being served in the kitchen now' I said.

I think he was still wondering where he was. Of course he didn't recognise me.

'Just bring me an assortment on a plate.' He ordered tersely 'No mushrooms.'

He obviously put me down as some sort of waiter.

'It's self-service, I'm afraid. I'll show you the way.'

'Oh, very well.'

I led him back to the kitchen, where as I'd hoped Guy was still stuffing his face.

'And there's someone here who's been wanting to meet you – hear your view… politics… that sort of thing. Guy Lauriston-Laurie – Gavin er…' and making sure Frank had a full plate, I hustled him away quickly before war broke out.

Part of me wanted to stay and see the fireworks but I wanted to continue my inspection of the house.

'Hope you didn't involve yourself in any stupid emotional commitment over Knocksting' I said to Frank.

'Well, not really' he said. I wasn't entirely convinced by his 'not really' and expected to hear more about this later.

'Tattie's in the dining room. I think she's found her daughter… Lulu isn't it? Didn't you say you'd played with her once when you were a child?'

So, with Frank settled in the dining room, I could continue my tour.

'Francis! We were just talking about you – come and say 'hello' to Lulu.'

Lulu, tall, freckle faced with what they call 'good bones,' smiled, put the dog down and came over to Frank.

'I think we met at the Show, didn't we?' It was the 'green wellie girl.' Oh pleasure, oh joy! Frank put his plate on the table and probably forgot all about it.

I returned to the library: it was peaceful. I could hear the faint sound of music coming from the chapel. The plasterwork I guessed to be seventeenth century. The cornice continued round the corner of the L shaped room and I followed it:– there were more well stacked bookshelves and a high-backed knoll sofa facing the window, in the uncurtained reflection of which I could see, very plainly, a couple cosying up. It was Rex and his Alice and it didn't look as if they were discussing how to make an opera.

They didn't notice me and I crept away along the passage and turned right up some steps and into a hall with a more formal oak staircase, which I thought would probably lead to the Georgian wing. Up I went, meeting an old guy in a brown velvet jacket on his way down, who looked at me quizzically.

'Just on my way to inspect the plumbing,' I said cheerily and took another bite at the game pie. I could feel his eyes following me, so I walked confidently to the first door I found and opened it. It was the drawing room – high ceilinged in total contrast to the other rooms, and was indeed Georgian with a magnificent marble fireplace and Chippendale furniture. Elegant, cool and mostly unused I would say, with pale green walls and a slightly musty smell. I reckoned the entrance to the tower must be somewhere to the left. There was a door at the far end of the room and I went over and opened it. The musty, damp smell intensified and I knew I'd found it. I picked my way over uneven floor boards, drawn as if by a magnet to a spiral stone stairway up to a large chamber on the floor above, swearing as I missed the last step in the dark and falling on my knees – the last bit of pie lost. I rubbed my knees, then, suddenly, a very faint light, which I could just make out at the other end of the room, seemed to be moving closer. I watched, transfixed.

'You OK?'

The voice made me jump but it was a guy's voice and now my eyes were getting used to the gloom I could see it belonged to a man holding a lantern: he held it up to my face.

'Hello... It's you! It's me... Errol. We met at Dundrennan and at the Barreough – you remember.' The light from the lantern gleamed on his baldpate. It was the frustrated archaeologist.

'What the hell are you doing up here?' I asked, but not in an unfriendly way.

'The whole team came over with Con – and I remembered your telling me about a family museum here. I've a helluva lot to thank you for, actually.'

'How come?'

'Well, I asked our host if I could possibly see it.. me being so interested. He's a nice old fella – really great – and he said, 'Come and have a look. It's over there.'– Errol wafted his free hand towards a number of tables and shelves– 'It's absolutely brilliant... the treasures... you wouldn't believe.'

'I'm glad you got to see it.'

'Well, that's not all. The artefacts are all jumbled up any old how, cobwebs, not properly listed and, I mean, it doesn't seem right to have a tooth of Robert the Bruce exposed to the air, does it?'

I said 'Probably not.'

'So I told him the whole thing needed to be sorted and conserved and he said that since I seemed to know so much about it, perhaps I should take on the job.' He stopped and I could see his teeth shining in a huge smile.

'And you said?'

'What do you think? And even that's not all. I told him about my job at Crass Dippy – organising, management and so on and the long and short of it is…. he offered me the post of general factotum, a sort of administrator. He's thinking of opening the house to the public and needs someone with some business acumen…. In other words – me! I'm throwing in my job as soon as I get back – fantastic!'

'I can see how it might work but you're sure you're not taking a leap in the dark? I mean – hang on, you've only just met the old fella.'

'Couldn't be more sure. I'll have pretty much a free hand. He spends a lot of his time playing with his old electric train layout – might make a good attraction when we open. You see that door? It leads up to another room – totally unsafe at the moment. He says he'll have it fixed up and I can live up there – brilliant,eh?'

He saw my piece of game pie on the floor and pocketed it. 'Rats. We're going to have to do something about them' he said in a proprietorial way. 'Can't wait to get stuck in. Go-carts, quad bikes, naval battles on the loch using model boats…. ' Ideas were tumbling out.

'Incidentally, how did the raft building go?'

He searched back in his memory as if teams and corporate bonding were something from another world.

'Oh – pretty good. Except we lost marks for paddling too close to some blasted fisherman. Talk about abusive! We had a horrible moment, as a matter of fact, when we arrived. Courtney thought she spotted him *here*. He caught her staring at him and asked her for a dance!'

'Well, I'm glad things seem to be working out.'

'Yes, and it's thanks to you, mate.'

'Why don't you come down and we'll have a drink and celebrate.'

'Great idea, but I want to check up on all these artefacts, do a mental catalogue.'

'Well, good luck, then.'

'Cheers. Who was it who said *Don't be clever, be lucky*?'

He held up the lantern so I could see my way down the steps and I left him to gloat over the collection like a miser with his hoard.

TWENTY NINE

Back downstairs again, I poured myself another drink and got into conversation with someone who was seeking refuge from Strip the Willow. The music for this reel was fast and light, inviting everyone to get up and join in.

'Have nothing to do with it,' my companion said, 'tantalising: like the sirens' call, isn't it? But don't be tempted.' He was a good deal older than me and he shook his head sadly. 'I remember some years ago being lured on to the dance floor by a plump girl in a black and white striped dress. I was twirled and whirled so viciously, round and round, that not only was I exhausted but I couldn't see straight for a fortnight.... The dizziness from the dance and dazzle from the stripes made me cross-eyed. Like this.' He duly crossed his eyes.

'Frightening' I said and meant it.

'... and to this day, whenever I....' But he swallowed his words and took a deep drink, the remembrance of it all obviously being too upsetting to continue.

I could quite see how there might be old reeling yarns just as there were old fishing stories, old battle legends handed on to the younger generation: tales of danger, bravery.

'Did you know this used to be the priest's robing room?' He changed the subject and went on to tell me that the Pope on a rare visit to Britain had been invited to a reels party here but had declined.

We refreshed our glasses and walked out on to the Gallery. The willow was still being vigorously stripped and I thought myself well out of it.

'Good spectator sport. Fun for the young eh?' he conceded regretfully.

Hell, he was treating me as his contemporary.

The dance finished on a huge upper – everyone laughing, hugging. No, not everyone, a pair of outrageously coloured tartan trews was tottering weakly away. Ben, supported by Tattie's aunt, looked white and exhausted. He caught sight of me and they came to join us and I could see why. As soon as he'd got his breath back he said 'Look, I've got to go and locate someone – make a phone call… work' he rolled his eyes. 'It was fun.' This to the aunt, spoken with a ghastly smile. She was being unloaded.

'How's the dog?' I asked her (hint, hint)

'Oh, he'll be fine with Lulu.'

So that was no good.

'Hello, Hec' she greeted my companion. Good, she knew him. I offered to fetch her a drink and would then retire.

There was a crush at the bar and by the time I'd

dodged my way back, the aunt was on her own, leaning on the gallery rail and shouting at a friend down below. I'd hoped to deliver her gin and go. Tapping her on her arm, I thrust her drink at her, but as luck would have it (don't be lucky, be clever) at that same moment the Eightsome Reel was announced. She took her glass, glugged down the gin and with her other, surprisingly strong hand, gripped my wrist.

'Eightsome!' She spoke with fervour. 'Come on.' She was into a negative risk situation here. I made a serious study of the gallery rail, hoping she'd think I hadn't heard but her grip tightened like a vice. 'Eightsome' she repeated. 'I always feel eighteen again when I do an eightsome.'

'I'm afraid I can't do it' I remembered our efforts earlier in the evening which I now realised were quite inadequate.

'Nonsense – everyone can do it!'

She led me on to the dance floor and, still holding on to me as if frightened I might make a dash for it, busied herself looking for another six people to join up with: I found myself feeling nostalgic for the bottles and cushions.

I decided to give it my best shot – I'd show the old Willow Stripper that at least two generation gaps existed between us. Casting my mind back, I remembered a circle and a chain and hoped it would be enough.

The aunt gathered three more couples and reminisced happily about a 'Thirty-two some' she'd taken part in once at the Oban Ball and remembered hearing a rumour of a 'Sixty four some' once. Another old reeling yarn, I guessed.

Frank was leading Lulu on to the dance floor, no sign of a limp – his wound forgotten.

I was just psyching myself up before the music started when Tattie floated over to her aunt and I heard her say 'There's been some unpleasantness in the kitchen.' I missed the next bit and suddenly the music started and I was firmly pulled into a circle, galloping round at speed.

I wondered fleetingly if a fight had broken out between Gavin and Guy. Perhaps one of them was seriously hurt. It would be my fault but I had no time to think, I was now being whisked the other way and fast. Then some little twiddly bits, another turn and then hurray, something I recognised… the Grand Chain! I negotiated that reasonably well and was rewarded by a nod from the aunt and, with her firm guidance, worked out the logic of the rest, even managing a 'reel of three.' It was heady stuff: we were high on exhilaration. The old became young and the young, younger still and we were united in feeling we all had a drop or more of Scottish blood in us. I even did some fancy footwork…. A solo performance in the centre of the circle and, what's more, I enjoyed it. I saw the point of it. The grand chain came round again all too soon and it was over and the aunt and I were hugging each other. I thanked her for her expertise.

'You're a natural' she said.

It could be addictive, this reeling.

One of our eight came over to me and said 'You've reeled in the North, haven't you? I noticed you 'set' the Highland way, Aberdeen?'

'Very perceptive' I replied.

* * *

THIRTY

I never did meet our host, though Frank said he thought he'd caught sight of him. Nor did I hear the whole story of the unpleasantness in the kitchen – being careful not to mention it to anyone. Frank said rumour was rife but the only solid fact he'd learned was that Gavin had been led away to rest quietly in one of the bedrooms.

We'd managed to prise Rex away from Alice Van Heck, who was actually staying at Stewartston as a house guest and would be working in London as part of her sabbatical, starting in three days. So he sat in the car, driving away from the party, in a happy trance. Frank was also highly elated and I heard a lot about Lulu – her past life, her hopes for the future, her favourite pasta recipe, as we followed the lights of Ben's car.

We'd nearly reached the spot where the road forked – one way to our hotel and the other to Glen Stramon. The reels music kept repeating itself in my brain over and over – not unpleasantly. A huge yawn, which I didn't bother to stifle, rocked back my head: it was contagious and Frank started.

'Hey, look, over there… the Holy Grail – isn't it *lurvely*' Rex waived a languorous hand over to the left.

We looked. There was a glow in the sky – a golden red glow.

'Didn't notice the power station before' Frank said.

'Football stadium?' I offered.

'In the middle of the country?' Frank scoffed.

Then, without warning, the Merc's brake lights came on and Ben screeched to a halt in the middle of the road.

Frank cursed loudly, justifiably, as he'd just missed altering the bonnet of the Morris. He heaved himself out of the car, ready to sort Ben out, but Ben was already stumbling along the road towards us – his face as tragic as any of the characters from Rex's opera.

'Oh, my God, oh my God!' he kept repeating. High anxiety.

'Make sense. What the hell's got into you.' Frank shouted but Ben, trembling, could only say 'Oh my God!'

It took a severe shaking of the shoulders and a smart slap or two across the face, administered by Frank, to bring him out of his shock enough to point to the glow and say 'Glen Stramon…. Fire.'

We knew he was right. Of course it was a fire. We could see by the cold, pale moonlight flames reaching up now through a pall of grey smoke.

'What can we do?'

We??

He was suffering real anguish as he found his voice again. It was his worst moment.

'The cats! My career!'

Well, it was to his credit that he'd put the cats first.

'Look, guys, come with me, won't you?' He was pitiable.

'Christ! What are we hanging about for?'

Frank told me to drive and took the keys of the Mercedes from Ben, not trusting him to drive with the shakes.

The Morris rattled along heroically at sixty, straining her guts.

'Oh my God!' Rex suddenly yelled and gave a moan.

'Don't *you* start.' He was volatile: he'd been up – now he was down.

'You don't understand.'

What was he going on about? I knew I shouldn't have been driving and was doing my best to concentrate on the road ahead.

'I think it might be my fault.'

'Mmmm' I said, thinking it would be easier to agree.

'You see, I don't remember what I did with my last cigarette.'

It took a moment for this to sink in.

'You mean…. You don't mean…..'

'Yes, the fire, the bloody fire. There, in that room, where we were practicing with cushions and stuff. I put it down, or did I stub it… Oh God!'

I couldn't say anything. We rounded a huge belt of trees and the whole horror struck us.

What had been a house was now a blazing inferno,

flames licking through the gaping, empty windows of the façade as if from dragons' nostrils. With everything parched after the heat wave, the fire had taken hold mercilessly and it was obvious that nothing could be done to save it now.

We staggered out of the two cars appalled and joined a small group of shocked onlookers.

I will never forget the noise – like the rushing and roaring of a mighty hurricane – a greedy, crackling frightening sound like some furious and insatiable beast devouring everything in its path, smacking its lips, making you want to run, and carry on running, in the opposite direction.

Fire fighters were on a losing job despite powerful jets of water trained on the remains. Masonry crumbled, beams crashed down.

A local had raised the alarm and police on the spot were trying to trace Mr Erskine. No success here either, so far. Frank had a word with them and someone came over to the stricken and trembling Ben, who fished a piece of paper from out of a pocket of his ridiculous trews.

'It's where he's staying. His wife's in Jamaica. It's his girl friend's flat. Oh God – I wasn't supposed to tell a soul.'

Poor R.C. A second let down. First his house, next his private life. But the police had no interest in this information other than the phone number.

'You speak to him' Ben said.

We watched as the fire was eventually brought under control but Ben had gone on a cat hunt, hoping to salvage something that might rescue his life plan now seemingly turned to ashes along with the house.

'Mr Erskine's coming up from London straight away. Helicopter.' we were told.

'Any idea how it started?' Frank asked.

I saw Rex grow tense.

'Aye, weel – it's anyone's guess at this stage.'

Frank, who hadn't heard Rex's outburst about his cigarette, remembered that Ben had mentioned some electrical work – rewiring or something – that had been going on in the house.

'Could well be an electrical fault or a break in. Mebbe we'll never know.'

Looking at the charred remains, I could well believe this. I heard Rex's sigh of relief.

After a while the spectators melted away. I thought of my hotel room, the shower, clean pillowcases, and wondered if I'd ever see them.

It was starting to get light. We sat in the Mercedes and poured some drinks, feeling like spare parts, waiting for Ben to re-appear – never mind that this was the guy we'd loved to hate.

He'd been gone a while and we were even beginning to get uneasy. Frank tried calling his name.

The damping down process would be going on for some hours and checks were made continually to stop further outbreaks or rogue sparks starting up another fire: There was danger that it could spread to woodland and acres of moors surrounding the small estate.

We dozed with the smell of acrid smoke in our nostrils until I heard a frantic tattoo tapped on the window and opened one eye to see an armful of agitated cats clutching tightly at Ben's breast. I opened the car door and he thrust them at me. 'Don't let them out of your grip for a second.' Gee, thanks a lot, Ben. They struggled and this grew more frantic as the sound of whirring helicopter blades overhead came nearer and grew to deafening proportions – shaking and vibrating everything around. Zeus, or it might have been Juno, vented his wrath for all this annoyance by scratching my face but my yell of pain was lost in the noise of the helicopter landing a few yards away. A second's quick thinking caused Ben to snatch back the cats and he went to meet R.C. looking every inch the intrepid-looking-I-rescued-your cats – and the fire wasn't-even-my-fault – hero with just a pinch of deference. This pinch grew to an abundance as a figure leapt down some steps. Ben faltered and stopped. What to say?

We didn't hear any of it but we could imagine: they talked together for some minutes and with the police and fire fighters, before coming over to the car.

Mr Big was not so much big as, well your Mr Average-height. Fifty, going on thirty. No urban suit he. His white Nike trainers below his jeans glowed, seeming to be powered by each energetic step. V.I.P. maybe, but blokeish rather than standoffish.

It was obvious that Ben hadn't mentioned us so, approaching his Merc, he saw a complete stranger at the wheel. Rex helping himself to another drink and me sitting in the back.

Haggard, half asleep, our tartan bow ties askew, we got out and Ben introduced us. I'm not sure he liked what he saw nor did he seem to be re-assured when I was presented as 'the– friend – who – was – an – architect – who – might – have– had –some – great – ideas – if– I– could – have – got – you – two– together'

R.C. turned his sharp, penetrating gaze on to me. Did I, with trousers and shirt covered in cat fur and a livid (and increasingly painful) scar down my left cheek, look a figure of integrity? And I'm sure I didn't look as if any 'great idea' of mine would run further than a hot shower.

* * *

THIRTY ONE

'Well, let's get the hell out of here!' R.C. said as much to himself as to us.

Ben threw the cats into the back of the car and tried to look efficient but it was Frank who nannied us along and suggested we do breakfast at the Gordon Arms and, after further words with the Authorities, a quick recce round the sad, smouldering remains of Glen Stramon and a call to Al Patterson, part-time gardener and now cat minder, he took the wheel of his car and followed us back part of the way before veering off to deposit Zeus and Juno.

So we had a few minutes in hand before an early breakfast. I looked at myself in the mirror in my room and planned some necessary repair work. A quick wash and a change into a semi clean shirt, a comb through my hair and a sticky plaster over the scratch and, hey presto, – well not a transformation but a slight improvement. I flung the bow tie into the waste bin.

Frank didn't want to hang about – we had a lot of driving ahead of us and had decided to stop somewhere at a service station for a snooze.

Ben, now looking faintly hopeful, arrived with R.C. (still glaring and frowning furiously – and why not?) and we all sat at a table by the window and wondered what to talk about. The fire was the obvious topic but it was difficult to know what to say. There was something final about it – the place had gone. 'Shame about the fire' or 'Sorry business' seemed inadequate so, after we'd ordered, it gave me a shock when R.C. plunged right in with 'Of course, the house was heavily insured.'

I caught Ben's eye for a fleeting moment: he gave me a slight nod, I didn't know why. Perhaps I was meant to say something so I muttered 'That's good' or 'What a bit of luck.'

'Exactly so' R.C. replied, turning to fix me with his gimlet gaze, scowling, his low, dark brows knitted together. 'In a way, this fire may have done me a favour.' He seemed to be putting a positive spin on it. 'Yes, I might even thank the perpetrator if one is ever found....'

At this point I saw Rex lean forward and open his mouth – was the crazy idiot wanting to take the credit now? I leant over and poured him out some coffee, which had just arrived, and gave him a nasty look.

'I'm going to start from scratch.'

What was coming? I held my breath.

'Glen Stramon shall rise like the Phoenix from the ashes.' His look grew ever more savage.

Did he mean what I thought he meant? Well, seize the moment – carpe diem – seize the day!

'Absolutely brilliant! Brand new house – to your own design! (Well, let him think so at this stage). A bold evocation of Charles Rennie Mackintosh, perhaps – traditional Scottish style with your own style firmly brought to the fore.'

'Exactly so.'

And Ben, as if on cue, chipped in with 'Like I said, this is your man. Glad to have brought you two together at last.' As if he'd engineered the whole thing, fire and all.

'Charles Rennie Mackintosh – my favourite Architect.' R.C. turned to look out of the window and into the distance – the ferocity of his glare not lessening.

'I totally agree.'

He was a man used to making snap decisions and no messing about and the meal turned into a working breakfast. I don't remember eating anything but my creative juices were spilling over. I think Frank mulled over his collection of properties for sale, Rex read his newspaper and Ben stared into space, just relieved that his schemes were back on track. We forgot them.

I produced my ever-ready sketch pad from a pocket and roughed out some ideas there and then... the gabled roof, my own favourite bold buttresses, square paned windows sitting deep in the walls. We seemed, at this stage of the game, to be of one mind. Inside – an easygoing staircase, stripped wood floors, stained dark wood, art workers guild metal work. I dipped my paintbrush in the hot water jug and got going with splashes of colour... That peculiarly bright Galloway grey, touches of pomegranate – yellow in the motifs. I could almost see it finished and I knew he was as enthusiastic as me – his fervour just as intense.

'There shouldn't be too much trouble with planning permission – it should sit very comfortably in the landscape.' I felt totally optimistic.

'I'd like a pavilion by the loch – multi-purpose place for picnics, showing films, plays, concerts…'

'Great idea…. Battlements?'

Rex, looked over the top of his paper roused by the words 'plays, 'concerts.'

'Operas?' he asked imagining, no doubt, his 'Circle of Swords' premiering in this setting.

'I'll make a feature film of the whole building project from start to finish. Make a fantastic television series.'

Infectious energy flowed between us – you could almost see sparks flying– and then Frank short circuited us by getting up from the table, scraping back his chair noisily, tapping his watch, stretching and yawning and saying loudly. 'Sorry to break this up but we've a journey to make, remember?'

I was like a child being wrenched, screaming away from its favourite toy at bedtime but I could see Frank's point and he was the driver and it was his mother's car and there was no point staying on up here at the moment. R.C. had plenty of business to sort out, so we arranged to meet in London the next week and I'd have to come up for a proper site visit soon. We said goodbye – his disconcerting frown still in place (I learned later that this was his normal look) and he and Ben left. We set off soon after (I having rescued my lucky bow tie from the waste bin)

Of course, I was on a high…., this was the honeymoon period….and spent the first fifty miles or so with pencil and pad working out some of the finer details – brackets, corbels enamelling – always trusting my first rush of inspiration.

We did stop at a service station and Frank did have a snooze, snoring comfortably. I didn't mind his snoring, being far too hyped up to sleep now. Rex closed his eyes – he had a smile on his face.

While Frank topped up the fuel, Rex went to buy a newspaper and read out an item on page two.

'Headline…. MELT DOWN at MOGUL'S MANSION.' There was a reference to 'Olympia' coupled with 'Torch job?' (Olympic torch, ha ha) and a sinister 'Arson cannot be ruled out at this stage,' with an old photograph of R.C. giving a bitter look at camera.

In the gossip column, he came across –

'Among guests spotted at a Reels party on the Scottish borders last night were 'It girl' Serena Price-Kettle, and 'Grey' Gavin Wallace-Gordon-Cowan (prospective and controversial Parliamentary candidate for the United Loyalist party) who was sent reeling after a dispute over a piece of game pie, sustaining a black (or should it be 'grey') eye and a bloody nose. 'Just a friendly tiff' insisted Tattie Shepley-Hepburn. We suggest for 'game pie' read 'game plan'

We arrived at 'Applegarth' and left prezzies – to use Tattie's word – for Frank's parents, not back yet from Africa and said a fond farewell to our (mostly) trustworthy Moggie.

We'd grown used to empty roads, big skies, and a more peaceful, gentle pace of life and speeding down the increasingly busy motorway towards London in Rex's car with Blur at full volume was a frightening experience. However, it gave Frank a chance to thumb through his thick wad of Agents' particulars and we enjoyed the thought of the 'fully restored, fortified laird's house.' (Had he gone for botox or a full-face lift, bracing himself up with his intake of Johnnie Walker?)

'I'm really serious about this, you know' he said, waving his leaflets. 'I've whittled it down to a cottage in Gatehouse of Fleet or a Manse near Dalbeattie and of course there's Upper Knocksting.' His voice was wistful as he said the last one.

I hoped he might forget the latter – there were too many things that could go wrong.

'I've never felt so much at home in any place – I love the whole way of life.'

Well, selfishly, I hoped he would settle there and soon and I could stay with him – I foresaw lots of trips to the area in the future, finding good local builders, regular site visits. There were still so many places I wanted to see there too – we'd only touched the surface in ten days…perhaps one day a wee holiday cottage?…. and Jane and Livvie would love….

We were approaching the Slough turn off. My head had been full of Glen Stramon and now as I was getting nearer home my mood altered. Some doubt and misgiving came over me. Jane. Was she unhappy? I realised that of course none of all the other stuff mattered a scrap unless we were together. Jane – she'd needed to talk. Oh hell.

Rex dropped me off. I watched him go…. An urban animal, quite at home now in the crowds and fumes, dreaming of a Wonderland and Alice. I'd see him from time to time – probably – a pie and a pint at Bar None. Financial empires might totter and he might be left with only the potted palm after his divorce, but at least he had a goal of sorts and someone to share it with.

* * *

THIRTY TWO

I looked through the window of our sitting room – the house looked cold, forlorn, empty, waiting and I fiddled for the front door key. I pushed back a pile of post. Everything was too still, too quiet, I felt like a stranger.

Dumping my bag in the bedroom – it felt less homely than an Ikea room set – I went round the house touching things – Livvie's toys and high chair, Jane's squashy chair, hoping somehow to bring some animation into them. I touched our new blue telephone and jumped with shock when it sprang to life with a shrill bleep.

I picked up the receiver.

'Hello.'

'Hi!' It was Jane 'I'm not in Argentina, I'm still in Vancouver.'

I didn't like the sound of this. Why the change of plan?

'How come?' And I didn't very much like the cool tone of my voice. 'Everything o.k.?'

'I've got something to tell you.'

There was a pause. So this was it – the next few minutes could turn my life upside down. I just couldn't speak.

'Chris and Anna said wait till I got home.'

Oh God – bloody Chris.

'Everyone's been so good. I've been so sick.'

'Janey, for Christ's sake – what's going on?'

'The thing is – I'm pregnant. I'm so pleased but I feel really ill – spend the day vomiting. Chris – Christina – Anna's friend, has been brilliant – helping to look after Livvie and she took me to her doctor. We're coming home in two days – no shortage of sick bags on the plane, thank God! Al – are you there? Are you thrilled – you are, aren't you? I am. And another thing… I think we'll go for the local primary. They can go there together and … Alex, say something.'

Again, just for a second, I couldn't speak… This time because I was so happy.

* * *